DEDICONFESSION

Okay, okay. I'll admit it. I basically follow Bob and the children around and write down everything they say. Sure, once in a while I get a burst of original humor. But these guys are marvelous material. One could write comedy on a regular basis just by taking notes in our house. That is, in fact, what I do. (I owe the french fry scene—in its entirety—to our son, Brandon.)

Yes, the book is fiction; I made up all the characters. But I confess that Brian is loosely based on my husband, Bob. All right, he's very much based on Bob. Okay, he's *exactly* like Bob, except that Bob has hair. (Bob made me explain this. He said everyone who reads the book will think he has a receding hairline just like Brian's. I said, "Right. Do you seriously believe that readers will think I have a frizzy permanent just like Andy's?" "At least they'll think you have hair," Bob said. I smiled. After all, it's my book.)

There. I hope you're happy, Bob. I have just explained the key difference (and a real crucial one, eh?) to all my readers, who I'm sure are fascinated by the miniscule variances between the husband in the book and the husband who, I must confess, has been a marvelous support to me throughout its writing. In fact, he has been its editor, contributor (*heavy* contributor), and idea machine. I dedicate this book to you, honey—full head of hair and all. Oh, *all right*! Bob is not heavy, either. Sheesh!

. . . And now, a word from Bob!

Actually, even though I do have hair, I'm nothing like Brian—except that I do worship my Joni the way he does his Andy. I'm so proud to be married to such a wonderful (and talented and funny) lady. It never ceases to amaze me that each time she sits down to write, I watch characters and stories unfold beneath her flying fingers—while she is answering the phone, caring for our children, and handling Relief Society worries. Okay, so some of the Brian/Andy situations are taken from our actual conversations. But fictional characters usually get to do more than their real-life counterparts do since the writer can have them do whatever she chooses. Even still, Brian will never have the chance to say or do what I can because I literally have the best of both worlds: I have Andy AND Joni—and I love them both. I dedicate their book to them.

A NOVEL

JONI HILTON

Other Works by Joni Hilton

Books

Published by Covenant Communications, Inc.

Braces, Gym Suits and Early Morning Seminary: A Youthquake Survival Manual

Dating: No Guts, No Glory

As the Ward Turns

Published by Running Press

Five-Minute Miracles: 373 Quick Daily Projects for You and Your Kids to Share

Tapes Produced by Covenant Communications, Inc.

Dating: No Guts, No Glory (condensed from the book)

As the Ward Turns (condensed from the book)

Caught in a Casserole

Around the Ward in 80 Days (condensed from the book)

Yes, most books have a foreword, but since this one is a sequel, it has a backword. In other words, PLEASE go back and read *As the Ward Turns* first. Otherwise, you may never quite understand why Andy was desperate enough to ask for Edith Horvitz as her homemaking director. See, Edith is as crazy as . . . well, I was going to compare her to something. But since Edith is the standard by which all insanity may be measured, it makes it pretty hard to draw a parallel.

And if you don't read the other book first, you might not understand why Andy would faint at the prospects of Lara Westin, her first counselor, planning Nick's wedding. But if you knew about the time Lara planned a fireside, you wouldn't even be surprised if Andy had recurring nightmares.

Or, if you can't get your hands on a copy of *As the Ward Turns,* you can always do the next best thing: just glance around your own ward. Everybody's there, you know. Only the names have been changed.

CONTENTS

FAMILY FIREWORKS

It's uncanny how the joining of two people in the loving bonds of matrimony can make the whole rest of the family want to claw each other's eyes out, but that's what sometimes happens when you plan a wedding.

It all started in May, when Nick—my younger brother who's been full of surprises all his life—gave us a triple shocker. The first was that his shady schemes and ridiculous stories were actually just a smoke screen to cover the fact that he was a top intelligence agent with the CIA. We thought we had him pegged as a second-rate con artist (Dial 1-800-Snake Oil) when suddenly he showed up in a military helicopter at our son, Grayson's, baptism. As a general dropped him off, he gave Nick a letter of thanks from the President.

Nick stood there, surrounded by me (who, at 41, can still be fooled by just about anybody), Brian (my husband, who had always eyed Nick with suspicion), my mom and sisters (who thought it was yet another scam), and my three kids (who missed the whole point and just wanted to ride in the helicopter).

Then Nick waved the helicopter and intelligence work good-bye and announced that he was retiring—with quite a nest egg, I might add.

The second shocker was that he was going to marry Zan Archer, one of the three women our Relief Society presidency had picked to reactivate—because she was such an unlikely candidate. At 30, Zan was a fast-track, corporate tiger—too busy for men or for church involvement. Neither Zan nor my brother seemed the type to settle down, until their lives collided and they simultaneously swept each other off their Gucci-clad feet.

Now they were like matching bookends in the library of family priorities. They wanted children, church callings, a picket fence, and a sheepdog. No more dangerous spy work for Nick. He swapped his trench coat for a lab coat. Now Nick was a partner in an international medical supply company. He'd still travel to some of the same places, but this time the most he could get shot with was a dose of penicillin.

As for Zan, she cashed out on her finance companies and established a part-time consulting schedule for herself. Eventually, she will have a completely at-home arrangement, so she can be available to the children (who, if they are anything like Nick, will need constant surveillance).

To thank Brian, the kids, and me for harboring Nick despite our collective hunch that he was a crook, Nick and Zan announced that right after their honeymoon, they were taking us to Europe. That was the third shocker; it left us all speechless (quite a rarity in the Taylor household).

Brian, sheepish (but not above accepting one heck of a thank-you gift), has been apologizing to Nick ever since for the cool reception he had always given his brother-in-law.

Nick, reformed (but not above taking delight in watching Brian squirm), has been lapping up the apologies and reveling in their variety.

Let's face it: when a guy shows up in a turban, promoting Pakistani face cream that smells like bass bait, and smears it onto Brian's face as he opens the door, he can expect a cool reception. Of course, shoving Nick into a thorny bougainvillaea bush and spraying him with the garden hose before he could get loose might have been a bit extreme.

Nevertheless, Brian is trying to redeem himself for every less-than-warm reception he ever gave Nick so he can feel worthy of the trip. If Brian's memory fails him, Nick smiles, leans back in the La-Z-Boy, and says, "Say... remember that time I told you guys I was selling Greek artifacts from a sunken galleon?"

Then Brian winces, recalls throwing Nick out on his trinket-filled pants, and tries to explain another lapse in his hospitality. Actually, I think Nick enjoyed Brian's previous outrage; it proved his cover-ups were convincing. He even admitted it was one reason he had asked to stay with us so often.

As for me, I was can't-say-no Andy, too guilt-filled to turn away family, even if I thought family was just one step ahead of the law. As the oldest sibling, I felt responsible for everyone else. The famous guilt that descends upon even the best mothers had simply descended upon me twice. Once when I was virtually raising my siblings and then again when I had my own three kids. So when Nick would breeze into town, I automatically put out fresh sheets and pillow mints.

Oddly, I felt marvelously well-paid for all this. Nick was taking me to Europe, and, by George, I'd earned it! As Brian writhed under Nick's generosity, I simply blushed and made exciting plans. Could we see Buckingham Palace in London? And in Paris, could we drink hot chocolate at Angelina's? What about Switzerland—wouldn't five-year-old Ryan look cute in lederhosen?

With the trip planned for August (when Brian, as a history professor, has his summer vacation), there was nothing to do but watch Brian try to redeem himself, and anticipate a marvelous trip.

Nothing, that is, except get Nick and Zan married in July. So, amid all the flurry of excitement over passports and itineraries, we somehow got roped into fussing over wedding cakes, florists, photographers, musicians, and invitations. Now. As you and I know, the down side to asking for advice is that you usually get some. But Nick and Zan forgot this universal principle and asked for advice anyway—from everybody on both sides of the family. This is the reason why, within days, the Archers and the Taylors were ready to skin each other and hang up the in-laws by their toenails.

You'd think a woman who could run three corporations could easily throw together a wedding reception, and you're right.

But Nick, former master of disguises and the genius behind every over-produced caper in spydom, wanted to be equally involved. That's why the minute these two clashed over any detail whatsoever, they turned to a relative for backup.

Nick wanted to release white doves into the air as they left for their honeymoon. Zan said those kinds of doves are strictly cage birds and would die in the wilderness within a day.

Brian (siding with Nick, if only to continue "earning" his trip) felt sure there would be a law against it if the doves were really in danger. Then Zan's older sister (The Dutiful Wanda, as she would come to be known) said the birds would not fly away at all, but would swoop down to eat the thrown rice.

"Oh, you can't throw rice, anymore," Zan's mother, Olive Archer, said. "Birds eat it, then it puffs up and makes their stomachs burst."

"That's an old wives' tale," Brian said, disregarding the fact that he was speaking to an old wife. "Birds love rice. In fact, keeping them out of the crops is one of rice growers' biggest problems."

"Then why do most churches prohibit rice-throwing after a wedding nowadays?" Zan's mother looked like F. Lee Bailey.

"People slip on it," Zan said.

"It's because the birds explode," said Grayson, our eight-year-old, having no expertise on the subject whatsoever, but enamored with the idea nonetheless.

Brian laughed. "Have you ever once—*ever*—seen a bird flying along and suddenly just explode?"

Grayson exchanged delighted glances with his five-year-old brother, Ryan.

Olive listened to Brian's scoffing with a crimson face and a crimped brow. "Why take the chance?" she snapped.

Why, I thought, ask any of us for our opinions? Why couldn't Nick and Zan just quietly plan this whole thing and then send us each an invitation?

As if reading my thoughts, Nick said, "Well, a marriage is a family event, and we want the family to have input here, so we'll forgo the doves. Okay with you, honey?"

Zan smiled. "Unless you really want them."

Sheesh! This was going to be a long eight weeks.

Erica, our ten-year-old, suggested releasing white helium balloons instead, for the same "up-and-away" effect.

Wanda looked at me with accusing eyes. "Haven't you told her about the *environment?*" she whispered.

Well, Mother of the Year that I am, I think I mentioned something about Mylar balloons and utility wires, but I must have overlooked the old *regular* balloon hazard explanation.

"It can cause a blackout," Zan's mother whispered, as if the balloon police had the place bugged. Her eyes held the same contempt as Wanda's. "Or choke animals."

"You know," Brian said, lowering his voice to match Olive's, "Andy is also responsible for the greenhouse effect. She sprays Pam on our pots and pans."

"And on the barbecue grill," tattled Ryan.

Olive and Wanda gasped.

"Hey—it was a household tip in some woman's magazine," I said in my defense, sounding dumb enough to try anything. Meanwhile, I kicked Brian's ankle under the dining table. He grinned.

Then Nick wanted "No gifts" printed on the invitations. Zan frowned. "I know we don't really *need* them, but ... I've always looked forward to a big wedding, and ... I've always wanted things that belonged to both of us."

(How any couple survives their engagement and actually gets married is a mystery that defies explanation.)

"You two will have tons of things you'll buy that will be both of yours," Paula, one of my sisters, pointed out, seizing the opportunity to save twenty bucks.

"No, I can see Zan's point," her mother said. "A bride wants to open wedding gifts."

"On the other hand," Paula argued, "gifts are expensive. And what can you buy two people who already have everything?"

"Well, if you ask me," Olive said, ignoring the fact that no decision had been reached, and changing the subject entirely, "you ought to print 'No Flash Photography' on the invitations."

Nick pointed out that few people bring a camera to a wedding reception. Then *my* mother pointed out that the photographer would probably have a flash, thus breaking the rule, and why have a double standard?

"For crying out loud," Zan finally snapped. "We're not wax figures! There'll be no mention of photography on the invitations."

Then Zan's father, Irving, discovered that our side had invited eleven more guests than his side had. His eyebrows lowered.

Olive sucked her teeth and shook her head. "Certainly the groom's side shouldn't invite more people than the bride's."

Then my two sisters, Paula and Natalie, began bickering about which one of *them* had invited more than the other.

Zan began scanning the list. "Who's Sergio Gomez?" she asked.

"Oh, he's the guy who did my front end last year," Nick said.

Zan was appalled. "And I suppose you invited your barber as well?"

Now it was Nick's turn to look stunned. "Felix has been cutting my hair for nine years!"

Zan started sputtering and the room erupted into a cacophony of opinions about who should and should not be cut from the list.

I, who had remained the only neutral region during this long-running civil war, had miraculously kept my mouth shut (not so much because I have excellent restraint, but, frankly, because I was too busy being Relief Society president to enter into the fray). For this reason, I was suddenly proclaimed the One Objective Observer who could be trusted to make decisions that offend no man. Or woman. (And bring peace to the Middle East in my spare time?) My unwitting silence had earned me the coveted position of Nick and Zan's Wedding Planner.

Well, the river of irony runs high in the Taylor family, and this time was no exception. I, who have plunged my foot into my mouth enough times to have athlete's gums, am the last person *I* would pick to bring compromise to troubled lands, but there you have it.

I wanted to say no. Then I looked at the angry brows and pursed lips of both sets of in-laws and I realized I had two choices:

Refuse to get involved and let this thing escalate until we all appear on America's Most Wanted.

Or... take over the reins and hope peace returns when the two warring factions can commiserate about what a knuckle-headed job *I'm* doing.

I lose either way, but that's what big sisters are for (so says Nick). And Zan, still in "career transition," insisted she needed someone to help with "all this."

"I know *I* certainly can't do it," Paula said, as if this were a group therapy session. "I'll be right at the peak of my PMS just before the wedding."

Natalie snickered. "Mike," she informed the Archers, "is Paula's husband. He says PMS stands for Poor Mike Suffers."

Olive and Irving Archer stiffened their backs and frowned. Clearly, they did not even discuss such things privately, let alone at a gathering of the tacky new in-laws.

"Well, I certainly wouldn't hire *you* to do it," Paula fired back at Natalie. "You hired a Hell's Angel to play Santa one year."

Natalie gasped that anyone would question her exquisite judgment. "He had a white beard and a big belly, and he did a beautiful job."

"He said, 'Be cool, Man' to all the children," Paula argued.

"Besides," Natalie said, defending her choice, "he was not a Hell's Angel. He was just a . . . a motorcyclist."

Paula rolled her eyes and glanced at the rest of us. "Hiring a biker to play Santa—is that incredible?"

Just then, my first counselor, Lara Westin, knocked on the door to drop off some paperwork. Good, I thought, Lara is plump and giggly, the cure for any family quarrel. When I opened the door, she could hear the debate still raging. I mumbled something about Nick and Zan needing some help planning their wedding.

"Oh!" she said, her eyes lighting up. "I have always wanted to plan a wedding—could I help?"

At that very instant, my knees buckled and everything went dark. The next thing I knew, I was slumped against Lara's legs, and Lara was saying, "Help! Andy's fainted!"

Brian held my shoulders as I opened my eyes and came to. I stared at Lara's calves and honestly thought, well, at least Lara has padded legs.

"You must have stood up too fast," Brian was saying as he stroked my hair.

No, I thought to myself, I'm just remembering the last time Lara planned something. It was the Fireside Gone Awry, an event I was *still* hearing about. She called it "Chicks at Church." Every time someone mentions it, I feel prickly little hives breaking out on my neck. Or, as in this instance, I faint.

"The good news is, Andy's going to handle it," Zan said.

That's also the bad news, I thought.

Lara looked disappointed. No doubt she had already imagined the rap singers and Chicken McNuggets she could have arranged. "Well, just let me know if you need any help, Andy. I was a caterer once, you know."

Ah, yes. The catering stories. I remember them well. When Lara was first married, she put her husband, Jerry, through school (and through a living you-know-what) by catering. She catered the opening of a dry cleaners and served licorice bent into the shape of hangers. Couldn't be worse, you say? Add one heat wave. En route to the gala, the licorice melted all over the back of Lara's van. Jerry scraped gooey knots of tar off that van for six months.

Another time she confused a children's party with a garden charity luncheon and took stuffed mushrooms to the kids (who found they could lob them quite nicely into the neighbors' pool) and brought sloppy joes and jelly beans to the white-gloved ladies in Beverly Hills.

"I'll let you know if I need anything," I said, as I hobbled to my feet. A tranquilizer came to mind.

CHAPTER 2

THE BAND WAGON

Within a matter of days, I was longing for the huffs and glares of the in-laws. Nick and Zan made our disputes look like the height of harmony. They couldn't agree on anything: Zan wanted white cake and Nick wanted chocolate. They were actually gritting their teeth as they spoke about it. It nearly took a government treaty to get them to compromise on marble.

Then, Zan burst into tears when Nick said he'd just as soon have a dessert buffet as serve a sit-down dinner. "That would completely upstage the cake," Zan said. "I can't believe how hard it is to combine our opinions."

I wanted to say, "Just wait until you remodel a bathroom," but smiled instead.

When I asked if they'd selected the music, Nick said "a string ensemble" at the same time that Zan said "jazzy brass." Then Nick said he thought it would be fun to have someone sing "Short, Fat Fanny." Just as it began to look as if the wedding would be called off, Brian (ward choir director and music buff) volunteered to help me hunt down some kind of suitable entertainment.

The first band we went to see had a bare-chested drummer with a pit bull tattooed on his chest. "I don't think so," Brian and I mumbled in unison.

The next group was an ancient string quartet whose cellist had a hearing aid that emitted what Brian later told me was a perfect E.

"You shouldn't have yawned," I said.

"I wasn't yawning," Brian said. "I was stretching my teeth."

Another band, whose angry, pink-haired leader could easily have been named Gadianton, had amplifiers larger than my kitchen. They were performing in a stadium and Brian figured he could at least pretend it was a football game.

When they started up, I felt my seat back vibrate, and we did not have front row seats. "I feel like I'm sitting in the engine pod of a jumbo jet," I whispered.

Brian looked at me. "What?"

I raised my voice. "I said I feel like—"

"Wait a minute." Brian took two wads of cotton from his ears.

"You cheater!" I said. "I'm sitting here going deaf, and you're wearing cotton in your ears?"

He smiled. "Want some?"

Of course I did. But it was still so loud, we decided to leave halfway through.

On the way home, Brian pulled into a service station. "Self serving, that's me."

I smiled. "Where would a band like that rehearse?"

"And why don't they?" Brian said, hopping out to pump the gas.

I leaned out the window. "Do you know what Nick and Zan need?"

"A proper diagnosis?"

"No, smarty pants. They need a band that can play *both* kinds of music."

"And neither one well, mark my words." But Brian promised to ask the music professors at the university, and soon we had it narrowed down to two groups that Nick and Zan loved. Wouldn't you know they immediately began arguing over which one to hire.

"When you check out the caterers, don't give them a choice," Brian whispered.

We were getting into bed, and I folded the bedspread over a quilt rack. "My mom offered to help," I said, knowing what Brian's reaction would be.

"A *diet* wedding? I don't think so."

"I knew you'd say that."

"Oh, give me a break," Brian said, his eyes growing round as he pictured the disaster. "I can just see it. Bran punch."

I laughed. "She would not serve something so ridiculous."

"She would and you know it. Instead of little mint cups, there'd be little cups of soybeans. And a rice cake wedding cake. I don't know why she worries about calories. She burns everything anyway, so it's impossible to eat much of any one item." Brian propped himself up on a pillow.

"She does overcook things, doesn't she?"

Brian rolled his eyes, then reminded me of the double ovens in her new house. For years she'd been using the top one for everything, unaware that it was the broiler.

"I can just see it. Grandma's Flame-Broiled Cookies."

"There's always Lara," I said, climbing in beside Brian.

"Great. Licorice punch. You eat it with a fork."

"Well," I said, "We could always have Edith Horvitz cater it!" We both started giggling, but we tried to be quiet so we wouldn't wake the kids down the hall.

I had the amazing fortune to still be working with Edith as my homemaking leader, and I made the startling discovery that every week you work with an insane person, you have more in common with them. But despite her quirks and bizarre crafts (which usually involve her trademark: hot glue), I really do like Edith. Her contagious enthusiasm always makes me more adventurous. I find myself being a kid again and enjoying more laughter than ever on homemaking night. Nestling close together, we continued to laugh as we entertained ideas of what Edith might come up with for catering a reception.

Edith, you remember, had built her entire house out of particle board and hot glue. Then she covered the interior with multicolor crochet. A few months ago her

house collapsed and she moved in with Rita Delaney—
the one who had used a dead cat for a visual aid once.
It worked out amazingly well. Edith's militant cheer-
fulness was the perfect complement to Sister Delaney's
cranky gloom. Then Sister Delaney's even more can-
tankerous sister moved in, and Edith was back on her
own—this time in an apartment that looked like the
inside of a gumball machine. Piles of little trinkets and
knickknacks were everywhere, all covered with multicolor crochet. It looked as if someone had crossed Pee
Wee Herman with a bighorn sheep.

There was no getting around the fact that a wedding
catered by Edith Horvitz was sure to include food that
would stick to your ribs (and anything else it touched).
The more I thought about it, the harder I laughed. And
the harder I tried to stifle my giggling, the louder I got.
It was always so hard to get Ryan to sleep; I didn't
want to awaken him simply because Mommy was
cracking up again. Stuffing my pillow into my mouth
didn't work. "Go close the door," I wheezed.

Brian wiggled his eyebrows up and down.

"I meant because I'm *laughing*," I said.

Brian pretended to be disappointed. Then, instead
of closing the door, he began tickling me.

"No—stop!" I pleaded, now laughing harder than
ever. Finally I could tell I was shrieking. I tried to slug
Brian, but kept missing.

He laughed. "I'm this close and without your contacts, you can't even see where I am!"

"I can too," I argued, still trying to keep the noise
down. "It happens to be dark in here. Duh."

"Duh? How high school!" Brian roared with laughter. "Where did you get that?"

I swung at him and missed again.

"Hey, with your vision, you could play the original
Batwoman," he said.

Suddenly the hall light went on and we could hear
the padding of young feet. "Mom? Dad?" Erica's voice
crept timidly into the room.

Saved by my ten-year-old daughter. Brian switched on his bedside lamp. "Come on in, Sweetie."

She was keeping her distance. "Are you sure I can?"

"Oh great!" I hissed at Brian. "She thinks she's interrupting . . . you know."

Brian threw his head back and laughed.

"Come on in, Erica," I called, pulling my covers back from Brian and sitting primly and innocently on my side of the bed. "Daddy was just tickling me," I said as she walked hesitantly into the room. I could see from the look on her face she didn't believe it for a second. Why does the simple truth sound so flimsy in this family? Then I glanced at Brian, who was rolling his eyes and making monkey faces.

"Yeah, right," he said, and winked.

"You guys woke me up," Erica said.

"Me too." Now a smaller figure appeared in the shadows. It was Grayson. (Amazingly, Ryan was out for the count.)

"Oh, honey," I said, and got up to give him a hug. I put my arms around both of them, then glanced back at Mr. Responsible. "Shall we walk them back to their beds?" I said.

Brian sighed and threw back the covers with great effort and flourish. I narrowed my eyes and stared him down. "This is all your fault," I whispered. He guided the groggy Grayson back to his own room, as I accompanied Erica.

"What was so funny?" Erica asked as I tucked her into bed.

"Oh, just the thought of Sister Horvitz catering Nick's wedding," I said.

Erica turned over and bunched up her pillow. "Is she the one who doesn't have very much hair?"

"Yes, honey." Edith had less hair than a Russian head of state.

Erica's voice sounded sleepy. "G'night, Mom."

"Goodnight, sweetheart." As I turned out her light and glanced back at her bed, Erica's shoulders were shaking, and I heard a faint giggling. "That is pretty funny, Mom."

Back in our own room, I paused before climbing into bed again. "Are you going to behave?"

Brian smiled. "You'll have to take your chances."

I sighed and climbed in. "The story of my life." I snuggled up to him.

"Oh, no you don't," he said. "I know what this is. This *looks* like snuggling. What it *really* is, is you trying to see me, and you can only focus when you're this close." He scooted away.

I inched up into his face again, grinning. Again, Brian pulled back.

"What is this—a magnet demonstration? It's like opposing poles!" I said. "I get close, you pull back. I get close, you pull back again."

"I can't focus when you're that close and I don't have my glasses on."

I wondered if Nick or Zan had thought to check out far-sighted/near-sighted compatibility yet. "And I can't see far when I take out my contacts," I said.

"What? You're going to take something out of context?"

I stared at Brian. Were we losing our eyesight *and* our hearing?

"I said my *contacts*," I clarified.

"Oh."

"Brian," I said. "Who in this world ever announces that they are going to be taking something out of context?"

"With you, anything's possible."

I scoffed. "You are unbelievable."

Now Brian pretended to be suave and sexy. "Hey, uh, thanks Babe. You too." He pulled me close and we kissed.

I stared at his profile in the moonlight. "Come with me when I go check out caterers," I said. "It will be like a date."

Brian chuckled. "Yeah, right. It will be like checking out those horrible bands."

"No it wo-on't," I sang, trying to convince myself as well. "It will be fun."

"Yeah, I can see where you're coming from," Brian said. Then he turned over and whispered, "Mars."

I pinched his ribs. "Pleeease?"

"I'll think about it. After all, I only exist," he paused for emphasis, " . . . to make you happy."

I laughed. "Good. We can go tomorrow. It's a date."

"Not."

"Not?" I tickled Brian's side and mimicked him. "How high school! Where did you get that?"

"Do you realize," he said, turning back to me, "that after all we've been through . . . with moving, raising kids, building a house . . . if we had to plan, say, an anniversary party or something, we'd never go through all this?"

I smiled and scooted into the curve of his arm. "I guess life teaches you the things that really matter and the things that just aren't worth worrying about."

"I'd say give me whichever cake is cheapest, whichever flowers won't make everybody sneeze, and whichever musicians will arrive sober," Brian said.

"Wellll . . . " I said, "maybe the cake could have chocolate mousse filling."

We kissed again and fell asleep.

CHAPTER 3

ON A WING AND A PRAYER

At breakfast the next morning, Ryan offered me half of a jelly donut.

"Yeah, okay," I said, reaching out to take it. Then, remembering the dress I had to fit into for the wedding, I said, "No. No, thanks."

Ryan shrugged. "Gizmo didn't like it."

"What?! Now you tell me! You let that dog lick it first?"

Brian's newspaper was trembling as he giggled behind it. Gizmo, the shaggy culprit, looked up at me from his post beside Ryan's seat and thumped his tail on the floor. Here was a creature that would eat a baseball, a piano pedal and the receiver of a phone, yet turns his nose up at fresh pastries. (Though I have to wonder about the genius who designed telephone receivers to look like beef bones.)

I snatched the newspaper from Brian. "You were going to sit there and let me eat it, weren't you?"

"Hey—you said you wanted to sample wedding food today. I just figured Ryan was the first caterer."

I smirked. "Well, we can't go right away, anyhow. I forgot that I have a doctor's appointment this morning."

"An Alzheimer's exam?"

I put my hands on my hips (the posture I always assume when I can't keep up). "No. I have to get my eyes checked."

Brian patted my shoulder. "Good idea, Batwoman."

"You two are, like, embarrassing me again," Erica said, spreading jam on a piece of toast.

"Trust me," I said, "it's not a term of endearment." Then I turned to Brian. "I just thought I'd get new lenses before we go to Europe."

"It would be a shame to miss the entire trip," Brian said. Then he smiled. "Hurry back."

"Yes," I said, "I know how anxious you are to check out the caterers."

I was home by eleven, and the kids had all been invited to spend the day at friends' homes. That left Brian and me the whole afternoon to stuff our faces with appetizers.

The first place we went was a little restaurant called "Ed & Pam's." We sampled some of the worst cheese puffs known to man. Even Gizmo would've turned up his nose. Brian muttered, "Obviously, Ed and Pam are divorced."

I laughed and pulled him back out to the car. "Next."

From here we visited a chocolatier whose photo album included glossy brown sculptures of roses, mermaids, carousels, and fountains. He brought out book after book, showing pictures of mouth-watering delights.

"When do we get to sample some?" Brian whispered, eyeing the truffles behind a glass case.

I nudged him to be quiet and kept oohing and aahing over the photos. Finally I asked the chef for some prices, and without even tasting anything yet, nearly choked. The smaller sculptures started at eight hundred dollars. I remember hearing that desserts is "stressed" spelled backwards. Definite stress.

The next caterer showed us samples of beautiful seafood salads, coconut-breaded shrimp, gleaming oysters and crab souffles. "Zan hates fish," I apologized.

"Hey," Brian said. "You could have waited until *we* ate some to mention that."

Caterer Number Four had a noisy restaurant packed with happy customers. "Looks good so far," I said. The chef led us into his kitchen and pulled a sample platter from a warming tray.

Brian's eyes danced. "What is it?" he asked, trying to be polite and not jeopardize his chances of eating some of it.

"*Suzej kar nitfket.*" Our grinning host motioned that we should try some.

I smiled and spoke through my teeth to Brian. "I have no idea what this is or where it's been."

Brian popped some squid-looking thing into his mouth, and I bit into a vegetable ball of some sort. We chewed for a second or two and then, simultaneously, began gasping for water. I have never tasted anything so spicy in my life. Not food from India. Not food from Java.

"Ho . . . ho . . . ho . . . " Brian kept wheezing as he turned in circles, looking for the sink.

A waiter handed us two glasses of water and we gulped to no avail. Tears were streaming down my cheeks and I could hardly breathe.

"Milk," I croaked. No one seemed to understand. In my desperation I began pantomiming someone milking a cow. Suddenly a dishwasher nodded and brought us each a cup of cream. We downed it.

All the while the chef was grinning like a new father, glancing proudly at his employees and nodding his approval. Our reactions were evidently perfect.

We squeaked our apologies and left. Sitting in the car, we tried to recover. "I feel like I just ate a volcano," Brian said.

"If that guy catered Nick's wedding, it would be a mass murder."

Brian took a deep breath. "Say, you were pretty good milking that cow, Elsie."

I socked him in the arm. "Hey, it worked, didn't it?" I paused. "Santa." Then I began impersonating Brian as he turned in circles saying "ho, ho, ho."

"Let's get out of here," Brian said, starting up the car. "I say we serve peanut butter and jelly sandwiches to everyone. At least the kids will like them."

I glanced at the clock. "How's our time?"

Brian pulled onto the street. "I'd say we had a pretty crummy time."

"No—I mean, do we have time for one more?"

Brian gave me a glance. "There isn't enough time in this world for one more of those."

"Okay," I said, thinking of the wild goose paté chase I had just dragged Brian through. "I owe you one."

"Four."

"Okay, I owe you four."

"Thousand."

A week later, when I went to a presidency meeting at Monica Baldwin's house, I still hadn't found a suitable caterer. Monica is my second counselor, the only woman on the planet whose figure actually matches Barbie's. Lara was there, and Phoebe Burnfield, our secretary.

"Come on in the kitchen," Monica called, a tricky maneuver in her huge home, unless you have a docent leading the way. I walked in and saw the countertop lined with food. An ice sculpture of a cherub sat nestled amidst plump strawberries and kiwi fruit, shish kebabs glistened in sweet and sour sauce, and juicy tomatoes were layered with guacamole and wrapped into bright pinwheels of color.

"I didn't want it to look as if I'd been to cooking school," Monica blushed.

I stood there, staring. "Are you kidding? You've carved a watermelon into Mount Rushmore. What is all this?"

"It's an audition!" Lara gushed. "We want to cater Nick and Zan's wedding!"

I sank into a chair, dumbfounded.

"Here. Taste this." Phoebe dunked a tiny, meat-filled pastry into some pesto sauce and handed it to me on a toothpick.

I sank my teeth into one of the most delicious hors d'oeuvres I have ever tasted. "Hmm ... " I said. "It's hard to tell. I'd better have another one."

Monica laughed. "I knew she'd like it!"

"Monica, how can you cook like this and stay so thin?"

"I only cook like this for special occasions," she said.

"Me too," Lara said.

We all paused, then cracked up. Lara was a good-natured tease about her ample weight.

I stared at the banquet before me. Despite Lara's track record, I had to admit this was pretty scrumptious stuff. And goodness knows they had low overhead.

"You've got my vote," I said. "But I'd better let Nick and Zan make the final decision."

We boxed up some samples for the happy couple, then munched on the rest during our meeting. That afternoon, I told Brian the good news.

"You're crazy," he said. "Lara will put Fizzies in the punch and you'll never live this down."

"Oh, she will not," I said. "I feel much better with all three of them involved. Phoebe and Monica will keep an eye on things."

He shrugged, absolved of responsibility. "Not my wedding."

Nick and Zan swung by to sample the goods, raved about my genius in masterminding the whole thing (hey, I am rarely proclaimed so brilliant; why bring up minor details?) and settled on the Presidency Caterers.

That night Edith Horvitz called. "I have a wonderful idea," she said. She always begins conversations with this lie. "How about a Yucatan theme for the wedding?"

Brian can always tell when it's Edith calling, because my eyes and mouth both lock in wide-open position. Then I stammer, "Uh ... let me think, uh ... " while I try to think of a tactful way out.

"Get some big ol' ferns in there, some parrots, a mariachi band ... " Edith had it all figured out.

"Oh, I think they've already picked the music, Edith," I said, trying to sound regretful.

"I have a tape of jungle animals of that area," Edith went on, ignoring me. "You can hear monkeys and everything."

"Well! My goodness." (What does one say to this?)

"And I know a Guatemalan lady who makes authentic tamales," she went on. "She can make four dozen for ten dollars."

I could only imagine what kind of tamales ten dollars would fetch. "I'm so sorry," I said. "Just this afternoon, Nick and Zan asked my counselors to cater it."

"Well, these tamales would be something different."

"Oh, if only I'd known," I said.

"You're protesting too much," Brian whispered. "You'll be sorry."

"Thanks anyway," I told Edith and said good-bye. Where did her ideas come from? Were they floating about the universe like radio waves, seeking out bent receivers? Maybe, I thought, Edith had what Samson had—only with Edith, her sanity was somehow related to having hair, and now that she was balding . . . well, you get the picture.

The next day, while the kids were swimming at a neighbor's pool, a delivery man knocked on the door to bring Nick and Zan's first wedding gift. (I foolishly offered to have everything delivered here, while they were buying a new house together.)

"Sign on number six," the man said, handing me a clipboard.

I had just finished writing the T for Taylor when I heard the large package squawk. I stopped.

"Did that package just make a noise?" I said, forcing a smile.

"Sure did, ma'am. I suggest you open the gift right away."

"I'll bet. And can you tell me what's inside?" It was all I could do to not think of wringing Nick's neck for having such weird spy friends who had undoubtedly sent some exotic creature to bite us all.

"It's a macaw," the man said. He smiled. "Could you finish signing your name, please?"

I took the clipboard and stared at my unfinished name: Andy T. Gripping the pen, I finished it to say Andy the Dope.

"Enjoy your bird," the man called as he hopped back into his surprise wagon.

I stared at the box and dragged it into the entry. How could I open it? What if the bird sprang out and clawed my eyes? What if it flew around the room, smacked into a window, and broke its neck? What if it just ate and hasn't been housebroken?

Just then I heard Brian pull up. Thank heavens, I thought. Someone else to make the decision.

Brian walked in and saw me sitting on a chair, staring at a box in the entry.

"Having a nervous breakdown, dear?"

"I'm thinking about it," I said.

Just then the bird squawked again and Brian jumped. "What's in there?" he gasped.

"In where?" I played it cool.

"In the box. Didn't you hear a noise just now?"

I looked at him with a straight face. "I didn't hear anything. Maybe you need a rest, honey."

Brian smirked and scooted the box further into the house. You could hear claws scratching on the bottom of the box. He pulled the packing slip off the top.

"Caged macaw," he read. "Well, at least it has its own cage."

That did bring some relief.

"Hey—it's from Edith Horvitz!"

That brought no relief whatsoever.

Brian began howling with laughter, fell over a chair and landed on the sofa, feet propped up on the back, holding his sides. "I told you you were protesting too much. She's giving them a Caribbean wedding whether they want one or not."

"It's not staying here," I said. Gizmo had risen from his nap in a slant of sunlight and was now creeping around the box, growling.

"You're going to let it starve while Nick's on his honeymoon?" Brian asked, still wrapped in gales of laughter.

Now I growled. "What if they don't even want a bird?" I said. "You don't give somebody a macaw for a wedding gift."

"Edith Horvitz does." He wiped tears from his eyes. "She is one amazing lady."

"Yes, well, I am not so amazing. I am not keeping this bird in our house." I tugged on Gizmo's collar, trying to pull him from the box.

Just then we heard the distinct words, "Oh, give me a break!" Brian and I locked glances, then stared at the box.

"It talks!" we both shouted. Then we lunged for the box and began tearing it open like kids on Christmas morning.

Gizmo took one look at his new, bright red and yellow roommate and ran whining out of the room. Inside was a note from Edith, explaining that a friend of hers was moving and couldn't take her pet bird along.

"Awwww..." Brian and I both said, as if someone had left an adorable baby on our doorstep.

Edith had slipped in a page of care instructions and closed with, "May your marriage last even longer than this bird. P. S. They can live to be a hundred."

I gulped. A hundred? Brian and I stared at each other. "Well," he said, seeing that I needed some comforting words, "We'll probably die before Nick and Zan do, so you don't have to worry about inheriting it."

"Thanks. You always know just what to say."

Suddenly the parrot piped up again. "How fat *was* she?"

Oh, great. A bird that tells fat jokes.

"Your butt's as big as a barn!" it said.

I cleared my throat. "How big a vocabulary does a macaw typically have?"

"About five words too many," Brian said. "I wonder what else it can say."

Nobody needed to tell us that we'd find out all too soon.

4

THE REAL MACAW

The kids came laughing and shoving through the back door, trailing scents of chlorine and suntan lotion. They kicked off their rubber thongs and ran into the living room, where they dropped their soggy towels and stared at our new guest.

"Wow—a parrot!" Grayson shouted, frightening the bird and causing it to sidestep back and forth on its perch.

"And it can dance!" Ryan squealed.

"It is not dancing," Brian said. "You scared it."

"This is totally cool," Erica said, kneeling almost with reverence at the side of the cage. "What does it eat?"

"Children's fingers," I said.

Erica gasped. I smiled and shook my head. Erica inherited all my gullible chromosomes.

"This is a wedding gift for Nick and Zan," Brian said. "So don't get too attached."

"Awesome!" Erica is a lexicon of kidspeak. "Who's it from?"

It pained me to speak the words. "Sister Horvitz," I said.

"Mom told her how great it would be for Nick and Zan to have a jungle-themed wedding." Brian was giving me full credit.

The kids' eyes danced. At last—their mother had done something radical and fun. I glared at Brian.

"Yes. Well." I thought I may as well squeeze some popularity out of the event.

"It's not a parrot, actually," Brian said, suddenly the authority on exotic birds. "It's a macaw."

"Can it stay in my room?" Erica asked.

"No, my room!" Grayson and Ryan both yelled, startling the macaw again.

It screeched. Then it proceeded to recite a list of words that would wither a microphone. Eyes round with shock, Brian suddenly grabbed the cage—and risking the ends of all his fingers—carried it out of the room.

I was five steps ahead of him, opening the door to the garage, where Brian plunked the cage down and tried to regain his composure.

"Did you hear that?" he said. "Do you think the children heard that?"

"I . . . they . . . we . . . " I was as flabbergasted as he was.

"Did you hear that?" he asked me again, pacing and wild-eyed.

"I'll call Edith," I said, trying to remain calm. "And we can just tell the kids—" Tell them what? I took a big breath. "Do you think they heard everything?"

Fortunately the kids didn't know what half the words meant. Unfortunately, they knew what the other half meant, and we had an immediate discussion about proper language.

"I think you should talk to the bird, not us," Erica pointed out.

"Good point," I said. "Or maybe I should talk to the bird's sender."

I called Edith. "We just got your bird," I said. "Interesting fellow."

Edith was thrilled. She then explained that her friend (who she'd met, not surprisingly, in a mental hospital) had been sent back yet again and had to give the bird away.

"By any chance," I said, "did your friend have a colorful way with words?"

Edith thought for a moment, then started laughing. "You know, Andy, I didn't even think of that!"

No kidding.

"So . . . when would you like to pick the bird up?" I asked. I wasn't going to leave any margin for error this time.

"Oh, I have to take my friend to the hospital tonight and I won't be back for two days. Can you keep it until that long?"

I sighed. I am such a sucker.

"I know it swears and everything," Grayson said over dinner that evening. "But it can't help it. And it might get cold and die in the garage."

"Grayson," I smiled as I spooned some pasta onto his plate, "It's summer. It won't get that cold."

Grayson twisted his face into a road map of pleading wrinkles.

Ryan, beside him, did his best to copy it. "Please, Mom?" Ryan said.

"Please what?" I asked. "I will not have that bird in your bedroom."

"Couldn't it just sleep in the kitchen, then?" Grayson asked.

I sighed. The only thing worse than having a red macaw with a blue tongue in the house would be to have a dead macaw with blue lips in the garage tomorrow morning. What if we did get a cold snap?

"I suppose it will sleep if we cover it," Brian said.

I wondered if there were such a thing as a bird muzzle.

The next morning a man from the local nursery woke me up to deliver a magnolia tree, a maple tree, two lemon trees, six rose bushes and eighteen flats of petunias. Mr. Nick Butler, he said, had registered for plants at the nursery, and folks had been pouring in to help the happy couple landscape their new yard.

"Which is still in escrow," I muttered under my breath. I backed the van out of the garage to make room for the wedding gifts. I guess Nick and Zan figured they had all the china and crystal they could use; registering for plants was precisely what Nick would think of.

A ringing phone pulled me back into the kitchen. It was Bishop Carlson. "Sister Evans had a mild stroke," he said. "She seems just fine, just can't always think of the words she wants."

Just as I was about to express my concern, the macaw screeched, "Ask me if I care!"

"What?!" Bishop Carlson was stunned.

I had forgotten that we'd left the bird overnight in the kitchen. "Oh, Bishop," I said. "I am so sorry—"

For once, his end of the conversation was completely silent.

"You just can't believe what it's been like here," I continued.

"That's not the reaction I expected from you, Andy."

"Wait—that wasn't *my* reaction. It was the macaw's."

"Because why?"

"Not because—*macaw's*." This was turning into a circus. "See, Edith Horvitz gave Nick and Zan a bird for a wedding present—"

"Does this have something to do with Sister Evans' stroke?"

"No, but it's about to give *me* one." I thought about how hard it was to find the right words to explain this crazy situation and wondered: Does this mean that someday I'll have a stroke and no one will even notice?

"So that was a bird I just heard?" Thank heavens Bishop Carlson figured it out for himself.

"It's driving us crazy," I said, praying the bird wouldn't treat the bishop to its *complete* repertoire. "Edith's going to pick it up tomorrow."

"Well, I'd sure keep it away from the telephone."

I sighed. "I'm storing it in the garage," I said. And as soon as we hung up, that's exactly where Ol' Blue Beak went. "Serves you right!" it squawked as I closed the door.

After I paid a visit to Sister Evans (whose command of the language was decidedly better than my own), I dropped Erica off at her ballet lesson and took Grayson and Ryan with me to the preschool, which our sisters had painted and refurbished as a charity project.

"Hey—I have a trike just like that green one," Ryan said. Yikes—I had donated his outgrown, yet beloved, trike to this preschool, thinking Ryan would never miss it—or see it.

"Yours is too small for you, now," I reminded him.

"But I'm saving it for my own kids," he said. (Such a forward-thinking—and guilt-inducing—five-year-old.) I closed my eyes and hoped he wouldn't ask to look at his trike when we got home.

I hurriedly scooped up the broken toys we'd offered to fix, and the preschool director helped me put them in the trunk. Just as she was leaving, Grayson loudly said, "Hey, Mom, how come you're fixing all these toys, but you never fix ours?" (Uh-oh: A variation on the old "Is that food for us or are you taking it to someone in the ward again" question.)

I glanced sheepishly at the director. "Oh, I fix your toys, too," I called back to Grayson, faintly remembering one incident with crazy glue and another with some string.

"Not very often," Grayson said.

I started up the car feeling like the worst mom in the world. Here I was running all over town for some children I didn't even know—and giving them my kids' stuff—while my own children were going without.

"You know what?" Ryan said. "I think I'll give my trike to this place!"

"Oh, bless your heart, Ryan," I said, then felt ashamed as I realized my joy wasn't in his generosity, but in selfish relief to be getting out of the Trike Cover-up.

"Hey—maybe I could help fix some of their toys," Grayson said.

Normally I would have felt deep satisfaction at having somehow raised such bighearted kids. But, in fact, I felt my conscience tightening around my chest. It's pretty humbling when your own youngsters are more pure in heart than you are.

"I have a confession to make," I mumbled. "Ryan, the trike you saw really was yours. I thought since you'd outgrown it, I would just give it to the preschool." I was waiting for Ryan to cry over the smashed pieces of his mother who just fell off her pedestal. "I should have asked you first," I said.

Instead, he grinned. "You'll remember next time," he said, parroting Brian and me.

"Yes, I will," I said. "And Grayson, I do need to spend more time fixing your toys instead of other people's."

Grayson gave me a sympathetic smile. "Actually, I think my toys might be too complicated for you, Mom." He was letting me off the hook! That little scamp was telling me I was just over the idiot mark, but he sympathized! (Also, he was probably right. I couldn't even play a hand-held video game, much less repair one.)

"Thanks for understanding," I said. My boys nodded and smiled. I could picture them exchanging winks in a rest home, someday, as I spilled soup down my bib.

Forgetting there was no longer room for my van in the garage, I hit the automatic door opener as I pulled into the driveway. Like curtains rising on the scene of disaster, there were the remains of Nick and Zan's foliage. The macaw was strutting across Brian's workbench, chomping on a length of lemon tree.

"Holy Calamity, Batman!" Grayson yelled. The kid was watching entirely too much summertime television.

I stared at the scene, dumbstruck. Dirt and petunias were all over the floor and the magnolia tree was stripped clean of its limbs, like a spear marking a grave site.

"This can't be happening," I mumbled.

"Hurry—close the door!" Grayson yelled. I pushed the button again and watched the door lower on a holocaust set that deserved a standing ovation.

"Nobody open the door to the garage," I said. Grayson and Ryan were already stacking garbage cans so they could peer through the windows at the mayhem.

"Get off there—you'll fall and break your necks," I said, sounding exactly like my own mother. Somehow I had to capture the bird before it devoured every present in there. On the other hand, if the cage latch didn't work, what was the use in returning the macaw to it? "You boys come inside," I said, pulling them away from the windows.

Maybe I could trap it under a laundry basket and put some heavy bricks on top to hold it still. Or maybe I could throw a blanket over the bird. Everything sounded scary, except taking the plants out. That's what I'd do—I'd haul them out one by one. On the other hand, what if the bird realized I was stealing its dinner and it attacked me? That beak looked like it could crack a baseball bat in two.

I rummaged around until I found a catcher's mask Brian had used in college. I tied a leather coat around my neck and put skiing warm-ups on my legs. A parka and some heavy gardening gloves went on next, followed by Brian's fishing boots and a motorcycle helmet. I was ready for battle.

Slowly I crept into the garage, praying the bird wouldn't notice me.

It noticed me. It cocked its head to one side as I hobbled my way to the maple tree. Slowly I dragged the heavy can across the cement, then hefted it up one step at a time to the laundry room. I felt like I was building a Nephite pyramid one block at a time.

"I *hate* dieting!" the bird said.

"Too bad for you," I snapped. Then I stopped dead in my tracks. *I am having a conversation with a bird?* I blinked. Did it actually understand what it was saying?

This bird had to go; it was giving me the creeps (not to mention the evil eye).

Just then the bird called me some things people get beat up in prison for saying.

How many Relief Society presidents spend the afternoon dressed like Goofy the Sportsman, hauling half-dead plants into their laundry rooms, and getting cussed out by a wedding present?

Now the bird was walking towards me in long, deliberate strides. Just as I was sure it was going to pin me to the ground and ask me if I felt lucky, I heard Brian's car pull in. Thank heavens!

All at once, the garage door started going up. I turned, a rose bush in each arm, and shook my head to signal Brian that he shouldn't open the door and let the bird out.

Suddenly Brian leaped from the car. "Hold it right there!" he yelled and ran toward me. He's going to rescue me, I thought.

Instead, he hit me like a falling piano. I fell flat on the ground and rolled over, the rose bushes hitting the cement and bursting from their cans.

"Andy—call the police!" Brian screamed in my ear as he held me in some kind of painful wrestling pose. "Call the police—*now*."

I tried to yell, but the mask was smashing my mouth. Brian yanked one of my arms hard up behind my back, dug a knee into my side, and sat on my legs. I tried to speak but could only grunt in pain. It wouldn't have done any good, anyway; Birdzilla was squawking loud enough to drown out any scream I could muster.

Grayson called from the laundry room, "Dad? Are you home?"

"Call the police—hurry!" Brian screamed, still deafening me. "Andy! Andy!"

"It's me!" I finally squeaked.

Brian sprang off my back as if I'd shot him out of a cannon. "Andy?!"

I snarled and rolled over, a bundle of bruises. "Who did you think it was?" I would have given anything at that moment to be able to reach a rose bush and whack him over the head with it.

"Andy! Is that you?" Brian scooped me up and carried me into the house. Grayson and Ryan scattered. "What are you doing dressed up like a burglar?"

"A burglar, Brian? Excuse me? This is burglar attire? I don't think so."

"You can't even tell you're a woman."

"After that ridiculous attack, that's probably what I'll hear at my next physical."

"Hey—I was defending my family."

"You were *attacking* your family. What on earth were you thinking, Brian?"

Brian was sputtering now, as he helped me take off my bird-proof helmet. "I thought you were a burglar."

"Stealing plants."

"I don't know! I thought you were cleaning out the garage."

I rubbed my sore shoulder. "Any burglar who wants to clean out our garage is welcome to it, as far as I'm concerned."

"And steal all my tools?"

"That's what you were defending?" I shouted. "Drill bits?"

Now Brian started shouting. "And I'm supposed to know that my wife has put on a catcher's mask, a ski suit, fishing boots—"

"I had to so that stupid bird wouldn't attack me! It's probably gotten loose, thanks to you, and it's terrorizing the neighborhood. It's probably eaten every tree between here and Beach Avenue."

Brian dashed back to the garage and closed the door. Amazingly enough, the bird was still safely inside.

"Why did you open the garage door in the first place?" I yelled after him. "I was doing just fine."

"You looked like Darth Vader," Brian yelled back.

"Mom, you opened the garage door, too," Grayson reminded me from his own perch on a nearby chair.

"Oh, just what I need," I sneered. "Witnesses."

Just then sirens blared as two police cars came roaring into the driveway. Four policemen leaped from their cars and crouched behind their open doors with their guns drawn.

From his lookout post at the dining room window, Ryan shouted, "Grayson, look! Policemen! Cool!"

"I cannot believe this," I said. "I'm going to kill Edith Horvitz."

"Who called the police?" Brian gasped, dashing to the front door. The bird came flapping into the laundry room from the garage.

I just closed my eyes and shook my head.

Soon four police officers were standing in the entryway, hearing what had to be the dumbest explanation of their careers. The guys down at the precinct were going to howl over this one for a month. Maybe they'd even take us to Tall Claims Court.

I stood up and tried to shake hands. Every bone in my body felt like I'd just fallen off a ninety-foot cliff. The policemen reached their hands out hesitantly, squinting at my clothes. I could see "nut case" written in every eye.

Brian was a fountain of apologies (what else, after weeks of practicing on Nick) and walked them back out to their cars as I slumped onto the sofa again.

"Andy," he whispered, returning to my side. "I am so sorry." He pulled a gardening glove off my left hand and kissed it. "I'd never hurt you. You know that."

"Yuck!" This is Ryan's reaction to any kiss, which I must remember to videotape so I can show it to his dates someday.

Now Brian took me in his arms and kissed me. This created Gross-Out Overload for Ryan, who disappeared into the kitchen with Grayson. Every crisis ends in a bowl of ice cream for these two.

Brian locked the bird in the laundry room until we could repair the cage lock. It had started eating his workbench, Brian reported, and I could only imagine what it was doing to the boxes of detergent in the laundry room.

Just as Brian was massaging my back and shoulders, the phone rang.

"It's Erica," Grayson called from the kitchen. "She wants to know if you're going to pick her up from ballet."

"Oh my gosh—I forgot!" Once again, I felt like the worst mother in the world. Brian tucked a blanket around me, brought me some ice cream of my own (okay, so *my* crises end with ice cream, too), then drove to the ballet studio.

We let the boys tell Erica their version of the event. Grayson depicted Brian as a true hero, who had risked getting shot by a potentially armed intruder, just to save his family. Ryan described me as looking like a space alien in a gas mask. Naturally, Erica bought the entire story.

Brian helped me into a hot bath and washed my back for me. "I really am sorry, Andy," he said. "You must have been terrified." (He was starting to believe Grayson's bigger-than-life description.)

"Mostly I was mad," I confessed. "And not just at you—at the whole situation. You know whose fault this really is?"

"Ours, for letting Nick and Zan store their stuff here."

I frowned. Taking the blame is never a comfortable course of action for me. "I was going to say Nick and Zan for getting married in the first place."

Brian smiled. "Ah."

I wrung out a sponge over my bruised knees.

"You know the real shame in all this?" Brian said.

"What?"

"If I'd only had a video camera running, I could have sent the footage in to the evening news. I'll bet they would have paid me forty-five bucks."

I turned to Brian, smiled, and put my arms around his neck. "You think of everything, honey." I hugged him, pulling him farther and farther toward me.

"Hey—not so hard. I—wait—" Brian was losing his balance now. "Andy, stop—"

I pulled once last time—hard. Brian tumbled into the tub with me, splashing and sputtering.

"Andy!" he yelled, scrambling to get loose. "I have my clothes on! I can't believe this—my shoes!"

"Oh," I said, feigning true regret. "If only I'd had the video camera running."

SAVING THE DAY

Wearing an old sheet with two eye-holes cut in it, Brian became the Ghost of Birdcatchers Past and somehow herded the macaw back into the repaired cage. Covering it up, he placed it in the kitchen again. "This way, if it escapes in the night, we'll probably hear it."

"That's right," I said. "It will start eating the curtain rods and we'll hear them crashing onto the floor."

The next day was Zan's bridal shower, and don't think I didn't give serious thought to hauling that bird over to the party to liven things up. If Zan weren't in the midst of packing and moving things into storage, I'd have delivered one brightly plumed turkey on day one. I might even have cooked it.

Naturally, there was a ward funeral and a birth the same day as the shower. I was in the kitchen early, preparing a casserole for the funeral when Steve Overland, the elder's quorum president, called. "Justine had the baby!" he crowed.

I had just opened my mouth to say, "Wonderful—is it a boy or girl?" when the macaw LOUDLY screeched, "So what?"

"Well! Suit yourself!" Steve said, and hung up.

"Wait—" it was too late. He was gone. Frantically, I dialed their home. Nothing. Steve must have called from the hospital. I dialed there and was told Justine was resting. No doubt Steve was making calls from a pay phone and I had no way to reach him to apologize.

I whirled around and whipped the cover off the macaw's cage. "You! You!" I shouted.

"A-choo!" the bird said. "God bless you."

I gritted my teeth and stared him down. Erica came into the kitchen. "Smells good in here," she said. "Is there a funeral today?"

I decided to ignore the implication that I only cook decent meals when there's a funeral. "Brother Andrews died," I said. And then, to lighten things up, "And Justine Overland had her baby."

Erica's eyes lit up. She can't wait to be a baby-sitter and has eagerly anticipated the birth of what could be her first customer in a glorious career. "What are they naming it?" she asked, her face full of anticipation.

"I don't know."

"Well, was it a boy or girl?"

"I don't know," I said again.

"How much did it weigh?"

"Erica, I don't know that, either." I was feeling sorry to have brought it up.

Erica frowned. "Well, I thought you were supposed to find out things like that." She shrugged and went back into the family room.

I glared at the macaw. Just then I heard the phone ring, but when I answered, no one was there. Five minutes later, the same thing happened again. For an instant I wondered if Steve was so mad at my lack of interest that he was calling back and hanging up just to get even.

I headed into the family room where all three kids were glued to the morning cartoons. Suddenly I heard the microwave beep, back in the kitchen. "Who's cooking something?" I asked. They didn't even look up.

I turned off the television. "I heard the microwave go off," I said. "Who is cooking something?"

All three of them stared blankly back at me and shook their heads. "Look. I want a straight answer. One of you isn't telling the truth."

Now all three of them began denying any responsibility.

Furious, I went back to the kitchen and opened the oven door. It was empty. "Okay, who turned on the microwave with nothing in it?" I shouted. "That can ruin the oven—"

Brian appeared in the kitchen just as the phone rang again. I picked it up. "Hello?" Another dial tone. I slammed the receiver down.

Then the microwave beeped again. I yanked open the door. Then the disposal started running. I dashed to the sink, turned on the water, and checked the switch. It was in the off position. I could feel my blood starting to boil.

Brian took hold of my shoulders. "Andy. Andy, calm down."

"Why should I calm down? Every appliance in this kitchen is on the fritz, and—"

"Andy," Brian was trying not to burst into laughter; I could tell.

"And just what is so amusing, my dear?" I asked him.

"You are not hearing a telephone, or a microwave, or a disposal. You are hearing the macaw."

My eyes bulged and I whipped around to confront the culprit.

"So it was you!" I yelled. This bird was a better master of disguises than Nick-the-King himself.

Brian led me out of the kitchen and sat me on a dining room chair. "You need to get a grip," he said. "Whoever owned the bird before must have kept it in the kitchen."

"Hell's kitchen," I said.

Just then a cat meowed and Gizmo went flying into the kitchen, barking. Brian pulled him out, too. "It's just a bird, Giz," he said. Gizmo wasn't buying it and was straining against his collar.

"So. Once again, Gizmo and I have shared similar rank in an I. Q. test," I said.

Brian was laughing his head off. "That bird is good, you know it?"

"That bird is bad," I said. "And it's going home with Edith Horvitz today. The very thought makes me want to throw a Thanksgiving dinner. And you can probably guess the main course."

Brian was holding his sides now, still trying to restrain Gizmo.

"It's not that funny," I said.

"Yes, it is," he said.

Just then I heard a doorbell ring. Brian looked at me.

"No, I am not going to continue to play the buffoon," I said. "You go answer the imaginary doorbell."

Brian was still chuckling as he opened the door. Naturally, this time it was genuine. But my feelings of stupidity were quickly replaced by ebullient joy; there stood Edith Horvitz.

"Got my friend off to the hospital," she announced.

And I know what pushed her over the brink, I thought to myself. One more day with that macaw and I could become her friend's roommate.

Brian helped her load the bird into the back of her car as I pretended to be sorry that the gift just didn't work out.

"Oh, no problem," Edith said. "I've already thought of a different gift I can give them."

No doubt.

"A case of glue," she continued. "Some stuff I invented."

Brian and I tried to sound impressed. "Oh, my," I said. Well, there's always one gift like that, right? For Brian and me it was a weather vane shaped like a cobra from his Uncle Pete.

"So what are you going to do with the bird?" Brian asked.

"Oh, I've already talked to some folks at the zoo. They want him this afternoon."

Be sure they put him in the adults-only section, I almost said. The zoo was definitely in for it.

That evening I sat beside Zan and watched as she timidly opened her shower gifts. Here was one of the most gorgeous, aggressive women I'd ever met, and also one of the least domestic. Before the shower, Zan had asked me to stay close by and blurt out information about any housewares that she should happen to open.

Thus, when she came upon a negligee, I smiled and nodded while Zan exulted. But if she happened to open a broiler oven, a Crockpot, or a set of whisks, I interrupted by gushing about the various features of this marvelous invention. By the end of the evening, I was exhausted.

"You know so much," Zan whispered later, as she squeezed my hand.

"Yes, that's why I get the big bucks," I yawned.

Olive and Wanda loaded the loot into their car while Zan ate almond cake with apricot filling. It was a perfect microcosm of the Archer family.

My sisters sat in a corner together, whispering about how many swag lamps were in the house and noting that there was too much foam in the punch. Again, vintage Paula and Natalie.

My mother was straightening up, throwing away paper plates, and shaking her head at the amount of sugar which had been consumed that evening.

And I, unable to take off my Relief Society president's hat for even two hours, worked the room inquiring about homemaking lessons, back surgeries, and quarterly reports.

Soon Nick and Zan would be marrying into all this, joining two families who couldn't have less in common, but who had somehow found a way to interlock their lives and look for common ground.

Either we were splendid examples of love and determination, or we were perfect candidates for padded cells. I guess you know my vote.

CHAPTER 6

THE BRIDE AND GROOM REVISITED

On the morning of the wedding, Brian and I were awakened by the phone ringing. Phone placement, like which side of the bed to sleep on, is a marital decision that Nick and Zan had yet to confront, though its impact would last for years. (It was unlikely that such weighty issues were on their minds just now, but since the pressure of being a bride was not mine today, I indulged in a moment of contemplation about this.)

The day Brian and I married, we spent a good twenty minutes offering each other first choice of which side of the bed to sleep on. When Brian finally picked a side at random (to get on with the wedding night, he later admitted), he took one look at my disappointed expression and said, "If you wanted that side, why didn't you say so?"

"Because I didn't know I wanted it until you picked it," I said. This made perfect sense to me; Brian found it absolutely ludicrous. And this is how our relationship has gone ever since: Brian makes a decision, I suddenly realize how I feel, Brian reverses his decision. Hey, it works for us.

It was the same with deciding on whose side of the bed to put the telephone. First, I volunteered to answer it so that Brian could sleep, his work requiring the brighter eyes and bushier tail. Then, after hearing my utter lack of attempt to conceal my irritation at being awakened, Brian moved the phone back to his side, where he has been faking a keen mental state ever since and insisting that he is wide awake to every early caller.

This morning the call was for me, and Brian stretched the phone cord over his face to hand me the receiver.

"I found a pig," Claudia said. Claudia Lambert was the one whose house was so messy that a burglar broke his leg tripping over all her stuff. It was probably the first case in history of breaking and entering, and then breaking again.

"Where?" I asked, envisioning Claudia finally digging through the years of laundry and magazines to find numerous farm animals on the bottom layer.

Claudia laughed. "Through that butcher friend of mine I told you about."

"Oh, yeah." I was waking up now and remembered asking Claudia to find us a pig for the ward luau in September.

"He should be plump as a pig by September," Claudia went on.

"I thought he *was* a pig," I said. This was getting confusing.

"Right," she said. "I'm keeping him in my backyard. So just let me know when you want him."

I promised not to forget the pig and hung up.

"I hope Claudia's got a pigpen," I said to Brian.

Brian looked puzzled. "I thought you wanted her to clean her house up."

I scrunched under the covers, giggling. "I mean a real pig pen. She's going to raise a pig for the luau."

"Good grief." Brian rolled over. "She'll probably let it wander in and out with all the cats."

A wave of worry washed over me. "I wonder if pigs ever attack cats," I said.

Brian chuckled. "Pigs are docile and intelligent. They never attack anybody."

"Ha!" I scoffed. "They did where *I* grew up." I didn't actually grow up on a farm, but I went to school with farm kids and heard enough secondhand information to consider myself an expert in things agricultural.

"Where you grew up pigs probably put on knickers and vests and did the polka to an oompah band."

I pinched his side.

"Just like Looney Tunes," Brian continued. "The only place on the planet where the dish really does run away with the spoon."

"It is not," I said, laughing but trying to be tough. "How can you not know about the pigs who attack and eat farmers?"

"Is this every breed of pig, or just the Ninja variety?"

"It happens to be sows," I said. "And if you fall into their pen when they have piglets, they'll attack and eat you. I know of three separate incidents of farmers being killed by pigs."

"Sounds like propaganda to keep nosy children out of the pigpens," Brian smirked.

"It was in the *paper*," I said.

Brian raised both hands in defeat. "Oh! Well!"

I punched my pillow into a back rest and sat up. "I can see that the entire opening scenes from *The Wizard of Oz* movie were wasted on you."

"What?!" Now Brian sat up, looking at me the way most folks look at Edith Horvitz.

"You didn't get it, did you?" I said, folding my arms smugly across my chest.

"Didn't get what?"

"How dangerous it was for Dorothy to walk that railing above the pigpen. That was supposed to be an extremely scary scene."

Brian burst into gales of laughter. "Right."

"It *was*," I insisted. "Everyone who knows pigs was frightened by that scene, while you were just watching and smiling and missing the entire point."

"Piranha Pigs. Coming soon to a theater near you."

I threw the covers back, pretending to be disgusted, and started to get up. Brian pulled me back into his arms and kissed me. "Women who know about pigs turn me on," he growled, kissing my neck and tickling me until I squealed.

"Ooh—you can even impersonate them," he said.

"Stop it!" I said, tears of laughter running down my cheeks. "You are such a brat."

Brian held me close, laughing. "You don't even know who this is; you can't see me."

"Well, whoever you are, you'd better not get too involved; we have a wedding to attend."

Brian sighed and loosened his grip. "Ahhh . . . the day I thought would never come."

I snuggled against him and lay my head on his shoulder. "It's hard to believe," I agreed. The weeks of wading through dressmakers, florists, photographers, and bakers were finally over. "Just think," I said, "In two weeks they'll be home from their honeymoon, and then we'll be on our way to Europe."

Just then the alarm went off, and the radio began playing. Brian gasped. "When I touch you, I hear music."

I laughed. We got the kids up, then Brian shaved as I lowered myself into a bubble bath. I watched my husband go through his shaving ritual for the umpteenth time and realized how much I enjoyed watching him perform this daily task. There was a rhythm, an almost choreographed motion to it all. From the sweeping way he covered his face with lather, to the brisk way he swished the razor in the water between strokes, its familiarity brought comfort and stability to my mornings.

Brian slapped on cold aftershave and I winced. He saw me in the mirror. "That's how God chose who would be the men and who would be the women," he said. "If you wince, you're a woman."

I laughed.

"But," he went on. "I have to admit, the best part is when it's over."

"Same with shaving legs," I said.

"But you can pull pantyhose over your legs," Brian said. "I try and do that, and people think I'm a bank robber."

I smiled at him. "Sounds like you have experience."

Brian pulled a goofy face.

"But we both know," I said, "that real robbers wear catcher's masks and fishing boots, remember?"

Brian had the grace to look slightly abashed. "Sore subject. Sorry."

I wrapped myself in Brian's robe as I got out of the bathtub.

"I guess you realize that I don't own a single piece of clothing that is mine alone," Brian said.

I giggled. It was true; I loved wearing his oversized shirts and his wonderful, big jackets. I felt slim and girlish again, surrounded by so much extra room.

"When *we* got married," Brian said, "they should have asked, 'Do you take this woman and give her your clothes . . . for richer, for poorer, for large or extra large. . . . ' I'm calling Nick and warning him. I'm also going to tell him that you don't truly become a husband until the day you carry your wife's purse for her."

"Like you become a parent the first day you double-tie your own shoes?"

"That's right."

The kids were allegedly getting dressed, but when I went to check their progress, I found each of them dawdling over different toys. "We're leaving in fifteen minutes," I said. "We cannot be late to Uncle Nick's wedding." I came close to saying, "and you'll go in your underwear if you have to," but I realized that this morning, of all times, I could not follow through with that threat.

"Look at this room," Brian said, standing amid Grayson's heap of collectibles (which means any and all trash items). "Grayson, you should definitely invite your girlfriends over to see how you live someday, because I don't think anyone's going to want to marry you and live like this."

Grayson grinned. Wanting to get married was the last thing that would motivate him to clean his room.

Brian, my meticulous husband, whose road maps lie alphabetically in the glove compartment, was still staring at the rubble and sputtering. "This is worse than sloppy," he said. "This is squalor."

Grayson and Ryan exchanged delighted grins, excited to learn a new word. "Squalor," they each whispered, savoring the feel of the word on their tongues.

"Grays—Eri—Ryan," Brian said, "stop swinging your tie." And then in the bedroom alone with me, "I never thought I'd be one of those parents with so many kids that he can't keep their names straight. It's lucky we didn't have five or six!"

"You'd be taking roll every time you called one?"

"You got it." Brian paused and touched my hair. "You look stunning. You're every bit as gorgeous as you were on your own wedding day."

I hugged him. "That's what every woman wants to hear," I whispered.

"Yeah, that's what a magazine article said."

I slapped his arm. "You are incorrigible."

"Thank-you." Then he swatted my fanny as I walked off.

"You haven't changed a bit, either," I said, smiling back down the hall at him as I turned the corner.

"Hey—I know how you mean that," he called after me.

CHAPTER 7

THE MOTHER OF ALL WEDDING RECEPTIONS

The wedding itself was simple and intimate. Due to Zan's recent inactivity in the church, there wasn't time for her to prepare for the temple. So she and Nick decided to have a simple, family-only ceremony at her mother's house, planning to get their marriage sealed in the temple as soon as possible next year.

But they both looked radiant, and Bishop Carlson did a beautiful job with the ceremony, telling them how to make a marriage succeed (while they gazed, oblivious, into each other's eyes).

A harpist strummed heavenly music, and fragrant blossoms filled the room. Zan's wedding dress was a glossy confection of lace and pearls, while Nick looked like a prince in his silvery tuxedo.

Olive and Irving Archer sat erect, smiling properly while the dutiful Wanda kept picking lint off their clothes.

My mother sat with Paula and Natalie, glancing over the in-laws' house and nudging each other when they saw something interesting. Although Mother had virtually disowned Nick years ago when she tired of his escapades, and Natalie and Paula hadn't spoken to Nick in some time either, everyone seemed to have lifted trade sanctions to get in on the wedding action.

I was the only one who choked up, dabbing my eyes and smiling as if Nick were my own son. Grayson

caught my eye and shook his head, embarrassed.
"Someday you'll be getting married," I whispered.

"No way," he said, yanking at his tie.

"Me either," Ryan said.

But Erica was swept away in her own fantasy as
she stared at the bride and groom. I followed her gaze
and remembered having the same thoughts when I
was her age: I would marry a handsome prince, wear a
flowing bridal gown, have a glistening ring placed on
my finger, and float like a swan off into the sunse—"

"Mom!" Erica whispered. "I think I'll marry a sky
diver and we can have the wedding as we jump out of
an airplane."

"What?!"

Erica beamed about this sudden plan.

"What about getting married in the temple?" I asked
her.

"Oh, yeah," she remembered. "Well, then we'll have
the reception in free-fall."

I sighed. Here I thought she was dreaming of the
day she would look as lovely as Zan, and instead all
three of my kids were sizing up this event as a definite
drag.

I could just picture myself as the mother of the bride
in a jumpsuit, parachute, and helmet. With my luck,
Brian would think I was another burglar and attack me
yet again.

After the wedding I hugged Zan and welcomed her
as my new sister. Finally, somebody sane in the family,
I wanted to say.

Then I tapped Nick on the shoulder. He turned and
swept me into a huge embrace. "I love you, Andy," he
said. "You've always believed in me."

I cried and fanned my eyes.

"Hey, I always believed, too," Brian said. "I just
believed a little differently than Andy."

Nick laughed. "I hope we'll have the kind of marriage you two have."

"Me too, Nick," I said, giving him another hug. "I know you will, and I'm so happy for you both." I pictured the two of them in a sealing room next year, holding hands across an altar and becoming a couple forever.

From the wedding we traveled to a lavish family luncheon at the restaurant where Nick proposed to Zan. It was a tropical setting with lush trees and a sparkling lake. Brian and I held hands as we gazed out at the garden.

Suddenly I heard a screech and stared into one of the branches. There sat—I kid you not—a red and yellow macaw.

"It's haunting us!" I hissed.

"Nonsense," Brian said. "It's not the same bird. And besides, even if it was, it wouldn't recognize you without your catcher's mask."

Nevertheless, that was one restaurant I crossed off my list, great food or not.

On the way to the reception, we reminded the kids of their one duty: stay out of trouble. Actually, Erica would be a bridesmaid in the receiving line with me and Brian, so it was Grayson and Ryan who worried us most.

"We're the gift guys," Grayson said. "We take the presents as people walk in, and we put them on the tables in the corner."

"Gently," I emphasized.

"Right," Ryan said.

"I think they'll do fine," Brian said. "That will keep them busy."

"And no snitching food from the buffet," I said.

"Only the children's table," Ryan said, one little finger raised to make his point. Monica had planned a separate buffet for the kids, featuring M&Ms, cookies, chips, and sandwiches, to keep them away from the poached salmon and apple swans.

"And don't eat it all," I said.

"Right." My little soldiers, saying whatever Mom wanted to hear.

When we arrived, the florist was just adding his finishing touches. He had placed white pedestals throughout the room and had draped huge streamers of pink satin between them. Each pedestal was crowned with a gigantic fountain of flowers, entwined with twinkle lights, cascading down on all sides.

"Wow," Brian said. "Kind of makes our little bud vases look anticlimactic." I laughed. Years ago at our reception, the florist had goofed and placed skimpy little test tubes (as I called them) in the center of each table, with a microscopic bud stuffed into each. It was probably the only science-themed reception in history.

Suddenly Zan appeared. "Oh, no, no, no! This is all wrong," Zan said, her eyes brimming with tears.

Nick held her as if she were dying. "What is it, Darling? We'll fix it."

Brian and I exchanged glances. One year from now Zan would react dramatically to something, and Nick would smirk, "What is it, Meryl Streep?"

Tearfully, Zan explained that the pillars and swags formed pathways in a virtual maze, and nobody would know how to get out, once they got in.

Well, naturally Grayson and Ryan plunged into the labyrinth to test it, whipping through the aisles and shrieking with glee as if they were at Chuck E. Cheese's.

"Come out of there!" I hissed.

The florist quickly moved everything into curves and crescents along the sides of the room as Brian helped. Zan smiled.

Then the photographer proceeded to take what must have been a billion pictures. Nick and Zan—the only two people with reason to smile for two hours straight—kept beaming even when it wasn't for a Kodak moment. The rest of us got so used to huge grins that every time the photographer dismissed us to focus on a different grouping, our mouths stayed stretched sideways in odd-looking grimaces.

The cake arrived, a veritable skyscraper of frosting, frills, and candy pearls. Pink rosebuds peeked from behind ribbons of white icing, and an elegant couple stood atop, as if caught in the midst of a glorious waltz.

"Wow," Brian said. "Kind of makes our Mayan temple look anticlimactic." Our wedding cake had been baked by Brian's aunt, who promised the most beautiful creation we'd ever seen. Naturally, we have not trusted her since, though we appreciated the thought. It was a boxy, three-layer cake that looked like an archaeologist's dream. Even the insides were crumbly and you can't get more authentic than that. Like I say, no field of science went neglected at our reception.

"Oh, no—this is terrible!" Zan looked as if she could burst into tears.

Again, Nick supported his buckling bride. "What is it, honey?"

"That's not the top piece I chose," she said. "Look how subordinate the woman looks to the man."

We all stared at the tiny figures on top. Sure enough, the man was in the dominant position, holding his bride in a dip as she bent back over his arm. (Not unlike the pose Nick and Zan were striking this very minute.)

"I think it looks dramatic," I offered. "He's supporting her."

Zan was not comforted.

"Wait," the baker said, and climbed onto a chair to reach the top of the cake. He pressed down on the shoulders of the groom, until the couple began leaning the other way. Soon the groom was tipping slightly backward, as if digging in his heels but falling back nonetheless, and the bride appeared to be throwing herself into his arms, belly first.

"Perfect," Zan said. We all smiled.

Grayson zoomed past just then, but stopped in his tracks when he saw the cake. "Wow... awesome!" he said.

"Thank-you," Zan blushed.

"Mom," Grayson continued, "How come you never put BBs on *our* cakes?"

I sighed. "Those are not BBs," I said. "They're silver candy balls."

Monica, Lara, and Phoebe were busy in the kitchen, arranging slices of beef and turkey on silver trays and popping little rosettes of butter out of their molds. Soon they covered the buffet line with a feast of culinary art. There was a cone-shaped tree covered with skewers of fresh fruit and orchids. On each side were tureens of rich sauces for the fruit. There were bread loaves baked into the shape of wedding bells and wheat sheaves, an assortment of cheeses stacked into the shape of a windmill, a crab mousse shaped like a leaping dolphin, tiny spinach and chicken puffs, a basket brimming with vegetables cut into the shapes of flowers, a huge bowl of shrimp on shaved ice, and at least two of everything else they'd shown me in Monica's kitchen.

"Wow," Brian said. "Kind of makes our mint cups look—"

"Stop that," I laughed, pulling my drooling husband away from the tables. "You can't compare."

"Boy, that's the truth."

"You know what I mean."

Then Brian pulled me close. "Honey, I'm only kidding. I wouldn't trade our reception for any other. We may not have had the budget to make it a coronation ball, but I felt like a king that day. I was sealed for eternity to the woman I love, and I *still* feel like the luckiest man on earth."

I hugged him, my eyes tearing up. "Wasn't that the happiest time?"

He smiled. "You were hilarious."

"I was?"

"Remember when we went to the hotel that night, and you thought you'd help and check us in while I got the luggage?"

"Oh, that." I had told the clerk we had reservations, and when he couldn't find them, I raised a big stink, finally demanding to speak to the hotel manager. "This is our wedding day," I said, nearly pounding my fist on the counter. "I assure you, we made reservations."

Now the manager smiled. "Name again?"

I had rolled my eyes. "B-U-T-L-E-R," I said icily. "The name is Butler."

Just then Brian had walked up, grinning from ear to ear. He leaned one elbow on the counter and listened.

"It's *supposed* to be the honeymoon suite," I said, my tone implying that they should certainly remember who reserved their best room, for heaven's sake.

Brian had touched the tip of his tongue to his top lip in an effort not to laugh. "It's Taylor," he'd whispered to me.

I froze in agonizing embarrassment. I had completely forgotten that I had a new last name, and was standing there like a ninny, making sarcastic remarks and spelling out my maiden name.

I'd like to tell you that I laughed good-naturedly and apologized to the poor hotel staff, but instead I shrieked and ran out the doors, hiding behind a potted plant with my eyes closed, hoping to make the whole incident go away.

Soon a chuckling Brian was at my side and spent the next half hour convincing me to stay at this hotel instead of catching a taxi and zooming to another state where I wouldn't have to face these same people.

"I wonder if Zan will forget her new last name," I said.

"Knowing Nick, he'll register under one of his dozens of aliases," Brian said, "and they'll spend their first night poring through the computer to find their reservations."

The musicians finished setting up and began to play. They carefully alternated classical and jazz numbers, exactly as we'd asked them to. Except for the inch of white socks you could see on the ankles of the clarinet player, I thought they looked and sounded perfect.

"Oh, this is awful!" Zan said. "The speakers won't reach the sides of the room! I wanted a stereo effect." And this, without question, was more like stereoesque.

"I know!" Nick said, Mr. Solve It. He then redesigned the entire room to be lengthwise instead of widthwise. All the pillars and sashes, the flowers and food tables, the band and their chairs, had to be moved. Now, instead of a wide focal point, your attention was directed to the narrow end of the room, where the band was able to place a speaker in each corner.

"You're a genius," Zan sighed.

Soon friends and relatives began pouring into the room, keeping Grayson and Ryan busy dashing back and forth with white and silver packages.

We formed a receiving line, and except for hearing Erica say, "I'm Erica, Zan's new niece" so many times that it began to sound like "I'm Ali-Kazam's noony," things seemed to be going well.

One fellow came by with the unnecessary announcement that I used to baby-sit him twenty-five years ago. Erica nearly fainted. This guy was definitely enjoying the perspective this was giving my daughter and I forced a smile.

"I hope they paid you enough!" the guy laughed.

I wanted to say there wasn't enough money in this world, but I reached across to shake the next person's hand and thus move him along, instead. Thinking back, I remember charging fifty cents an hour. I must have been out of my mind.

"I was born the year the Beatles came out," the fellow went on.

As he moved down the line, Erica whispered, "What beetles?" I knew she was picturing a cricket-style plague.

"The Beatles," I said, "were a rock group."

Erica wrinkled her nose. "How come I've never heard of them?"

"Because it was before recorded history," I said.

Erica smirked. "Hey... what happened the year I was born?"

I thought for a minute. "I think that was the year all the cars started to look alike."

Erica opened her mouth to demand something more substantial, but guests were moving through the line, and soon she was engrossed in a flutter of compliments about her dress.

Dozens of Nick's CIA friends came through the line. None of them introduced themselves as such, but I could tell from the same adventurous glint in their eyes that these guys were not the accountants and bankers they were all claiming to be.

When the bishop came through the line, Erica complimented him on his tie. "Why thanks," he said. "I like strokes like that." Then he asked me for an quick update on Sister Evans before moving down the line.

Next was Evelyn Hooley, second runner-up in the Rita Delaney Grumbling Sweepstakes. Rita was bluntly critical, whereas Evelyn Hooley just questioned everything and shook her head.

"You know," Evelyn whispered to me, adjusting her hearing aid, "I'm aware that Sister Evans' stroke wasn't serious, but I think it was in poor taste for Bishop Carlson to say he likes strokes like that."

"Oh, that's not what he meant!" I said and did my best to explain the situation. Sister Hooley couldn't hear me over the music and conversation of the guests, and Erica was giggling right in Sister Hooley's face throughout my explanation, which didn't help matters. Finally I think we got it sorted out.

Then Brian's Uncle Pete, the one who lives on a sailboat, came by wearing his captain's hat. He was with Jelly, his long-time girlfriend. Jelly's name is actually Angelica, but—pardon the pun—a nickname like that is hard to shake.

"You know," Uncle Pete said, "this week is our seventeenth anniversary."

"Oh, congratulations," I murmured, shaking Jelly's hand.

"How about that, in this day and age?" Uncle Pete went on. "Seventeen years!"

"But Uncle Pete," Brian said. "You're not even married."

"Oh, but to be together this long ... you know how Hollywood is ... " Jelly said.

"Jelly, you don't live in Hollywood," Brian said.

I hugged them and moved them both along in the line toward Natalie and Paula.

"What are they celebrating—" Brian said, "—that they've been going to movies for seventeen years? They don't even live near each other!"

"Brian—"

"It's a twenty-minute drive!"

"All right!" I said and motioned him to keep his voice down.

Brian shook his head as Uncle Pete moved down the line. "X-ray Christmas cards," he muttered. Last year Uncle Pete had sent photo Christmas cards, but instead of a cute snapshot, he'd decided to share his chest X ray, crossing out "ray" and changing it to Xmas, then writing "Merry" above it.

"Look!" Brian said, turning his attention to the beginning of the line. "Now there's a man secure in his masculinity."

I followed his stare and saw Brother Wilkerson wearing cowboy boots and a tool belt. "Shh!" I said to Brian, "not one wisecrack."

"Who wears a tool belt to a wedding reception?" he whispered back.

"Just, please," I said. "And anyway, his outfit is nothing compared to Edith's."

We stared across the room as Edith Horvitz entered. She was wearing a dress, a cape, and a hat made entirely of multicolor crochet. There was even a crocheted feather stuck in the hat.

"Now I've seen everything," Brian said. "A yarn musketeer."

"Oh, dear," I said. "*Please* don't say anything."

Brian smiled. "Certain situations speak for themselves."

Just then my visiting teacher, Betty Carroll, came through the line and asked me if she could count this as a visit.

"Afraid not," I said. "Why don't you call me sometime, or come over?"

She pinched my cheeks. "You're so cute," she said and moved on.

I turned to Brian and laughed. "She might just as well have said, 'Fat Chance.'"

Just then we heard Rita Delaney asking Zan what kind of birth control she was planning to use.

"Excuse me?" Zan sputtered. Even Nick looked stunned.

"Margaret Mead would've loved this," Brian whispered.

"Shh!" Then I raised my voice. "Oh, Sister Delaney!" I called, mentally scrambling for some excuse to interrupt her. "I see your old roommate, Edith, is here!"

Rita looked around, saw Edith, and waved. "I gave her the idea for that outfit," she said.

"And she admits it?" Brian whispered.

"But we don't appreciate being called old," she continued, staring me down.

I cringed. "Oh, I didn't mean it that way," I tried to apologize.

Seeing her pal, Edith came striding like a macaw toward Rita Delaney. "You like it?" she said and twirled around.

"You'll upstage the bride," Rita whispered, and they giggled. Brian rolled his eyes.

"Brian Taylor," Edith said, cutting into the line, "why don't you wear a toupee?"

"Why doesn't *she*?" Brian hissed in my ear. I smiled and chewed my cheeks so I wouldn't laugh.

"I like my head just the way it is, Sister Horvitz," Brian said. So did I. Brian's hair had started thinning in college, but he looked as handsome as ever to me.

"Have you ever tried one?" Edith was not going to give up.

Brian sighed. "Years ago, just for fun. But you never know when a stiff wind is going to come up, Sister Horvitz." He began reaching for the next person's hand, hoping Edith would get elbowed on down the line. Brian began greeting the next person, and Sister Horvitz shrugged. Calling back to me, she said, "I hope you try the tamales I brought."

"What?!" She brought those ten-dollar tamales after all?

As soon as the line broke to mingle about, I dashed to the kitchen. "What's this about Edith bringing tamales?"

"Oh, she said they were authentic, so I let her put them out," Lara said. Lara would let you paint her car with a broom if you said it was made from authentic boar bristle.

Erica went off with some friends while Brian and I made our way through the buffet line to the tamales. "You taste one," I whispered.

Brian smiled. "*You* taste one."

Finally we each took one, then sat down with Monica's husband, Art, at a nearby table. I noticed that Art had taken one, too.

Brian cut into his. *Clink!* He put his knife in a different spot. Again, it clinked as he cut into the tamale.

"Try yours," he said.

I stuck my fork in and hit something hard. Pulling at it with the fork, I found a chicken bone and gasped.

Art was watching this travesty and began poking his tamale, also producing the same clinking sounds we had.

"There's a bone in here," Art gasped. "Well, I see that Monica's cooking school was money well spent."

Brian pulled a bone from his as well. We can't serve these," he said, and carried the tray back into the kitchen. Edith saw him and was right on his heels. I followed.

"Hey—where are you taking those?" Edith asked.

She had Brian in a corner. "Well . . ." Brian said, "There are chicken bones in those tamales."

"Of course there are!" Edith snapped. "That's how you know they're authentic." Then she muttered, "And you call yourself a history professor." She snatched the tray from Brian and plunked it back onto the serving table. "Those bones are a tradition," she said. "I forget what, but they mean something."

"They mean lawsuit," Brian said. "You look up 'fiasco' in the dictionary and you'll find a picture of those tamales."

Edith squinted at Brain, ignoring his protests. "You," she said, pointing a finger at him, "have no sense of adventure."

Speechless and sputtering, Brian sat down again. "How can she say that?" he finally whispered. "Look who I married!"

I stared at the buffet line, watching to see who would take a tamale and trying to guess which guests might sue us. But then I smiled: With Edith standing there in that hat and cape, telling everyone to take one, she was insuring that no one would! People were just smiling politely and moving right past the Twilight Tamale Zone.

My mother walked up just then and whispered, "I gave them something Christmasy. You don't think I was being too optimistic, do you? I mean, it should last four months, don't you think?"

"Good grief, Mother," I whispered. Thank heavens Nick and Zan couldn't hear her.

Soon Zan was ready to throw her gorgeous bouquet, but as she tossed it into the air, it landed on one of the wide satin streamers overhead. Zan looked ready to cry again, but Nick came to the rescue by yanking on one of the streamer ends which hung down from the center of the ceiling. Suddenly the entire canopy of streamers fell like a fluttering parachute, covering the guests and wrapping us all in peony pink. The bouquet sailed perfectly into Wanda's hands.

Zan threw her arms around Nick. "Beautiful!" she exclaimed.

And, I thought, it will also save the clean-up crew a lot of time.

Just as Nick and Zan were going to leave for their honeymoon, Ryan stepped proudly forward and handed Zan a pile of envelopes. "Here you go, Aunt Zan," he said. "I gathered them all up for you so you won't lose a single one!"

Nick and Zan both stood there, mortified. Now they would never know which person gave which present. The laughter of the satin-covered guests now turned to groans of sympathy.

"Uh, ours is the biggest, most expensive, heavy, silver..." Brian said, eliciting some laughter.

Ryan looked pale, and I knew he must be wondering what he'd done wrong.

"I'll call and tell you what mine was," someone shouted. Soon everyone in the room was promising to do the same, and Zan breathed a sigh of relief.

Then, noticing Ryan's quivering lip, she grinned and swept him into a giant hug. "Thank-you, my little helper. You were wonderful."

"Classy lady," I whispered to Brian. She might sweat the small stuff, but when it comes to the things that matter most, Zan is world-class.

CHAPTER 8

THE WALLS HAVE EARS AND EYES

A week later, as the new Mr. and Mrs. Butler were enjoying a honeymoon safari in Kenya, I was busting some dust under the living room sofa. Ours is a family of contrasts, and I always do my part.

That's when Brother Laird called. He's the one who videotaped Nick and Zan's wedding reception. "You can see the video now," he said, "and I've sent part of it in to 'America's Funniest Home Videos.'"

"Oh—you mean when the canopy fell on everybody?"

"No; I had already turned off the camera when that happened."

I closed my eyes. What had he captured—a length of toilet paper trailing out from behind my dress? Ryan taking all the envelopes off the presents? Or Brian trying to cut through one of Edith's tamales? I usually laugh at times like this and hope the other person is only kidding. But something in Brother Laird's tone told me he wasn't.

I cleared my throat. "What's on the video?"

"Why don't I bring it over tonight and surprise you?" he said.

This kind of suspense I did not need, but I asked him to come at 7:30 anyway. That left me the whole day to worry.

Worry, and move plants. While Nick and Zan had been riding happily along through an African jungle, I had been living in one all my own. Their friends continued to send bushes and trees, which finally outgrew the garage and spread into the house. It looked like a giant terrarium.

Just as I scooted enough of them aside to make a path for Brother Laird, a delivery man came with more. "Wow, you must really like plants," he said.

I gritted my teeth. "Love them," I said and signed for another cypress.

After taking Erica to ballet, Ryan to T-ball, and Grayson to a Cub Scout activity, I decided to do a little Relief Society work and called our new visiting teaching coordinator, Mavis Cunningham. Mavis is one of those women who come to mind when you're asked whom you most admire. She's the grand dame of organized pantries, the one whose kids all turned out perfect, the temple worker who makes you feel like you're visiting heaven, and the woman you'd love to be like someday.

We needed to assign a new visiting teacher to Ruby Fenwick, an agoraphobiac who won't let anyone in. For years, another recluse in the ward had been writing to Sister Fenwick (probably assigned because they had something in common), but now Sister Fenwick's husband was dying, and she'd soon need someone to coordinate the funeral for her—and a fellow agoraphobiac suddenly seemed like the worst of all possible choices. Also, we needed to assign new visiting teachers to three women whose visiting teachers had just moved.

We were just discussing all this when my second telephone line rang. "Can you hold on a minute, Mavis?" I asked her, and reached over my papers to press the hold button, then pressed line two.

It was Brian. "You looked like one hot fox this morning," he whispered in a sexy, throaty voice.

I giggled. I have to admit, I love it when Brian makes these calls. "I have you on conference call," I said, just to rattle him (though I'm a lousy liar and this never works).

"So ... tonight, you and me, heh, heh, heh—" Brian went on.

"Hmmmmmmmm. . . . " I said, sounding interested, but playing hard to get.

"Excuse me, but I'm still on the line," Mavis said, her voice trembling.

My eyes nearly jumped out of their sockets. "Mavis?!" I squeaked, glancing at the phone to see that I had in fact pressed the conference button after all. Mavis was listening to everything while I thought I had her on hold!

"I thought I'd better speak up before it went any further," she said timidly.

"Oh, oh!" I yelped as if someone were kicking me in the shins. "Mavis, I'll call you right back, okay?"

"Whenever you're through," Mavis said, trying to accommodate.

Through with what—being an idiot? After Mavis hung up, I groaned into the receiver. "Brian, I thought I put her on hold, I swear! I could just die."

Brian was laughing, enjoying my embarrassment.

Of all people to have on the line, why did I have to be speaking to Mavis Cunningham? "Brian, this is not funny," I said.

"I'll bet your face is as red as a beet," Brian laughed.

"My entire body is red," I snarled. "I can never face that woman again."

"What are you afraid of? After all, we are married and we have three kids, Andy. I'm sure the whole ward has figured out—"

"But they don't have to hear the prelude!" I shouted, pulling the phone cord along as I paced. "I'll bet she's telling her husband this very minute and now every time I look at him I'll know what he's thinking."

"Look. Calm down and call her back or she'll really begin to wonder about you."

"Right. I've got to call her back immediately."

"Just remember," Brian said, "it could have been a lot worse."

I cringed, remembering even racier calls he'd made. "So don't worry," he said.

"Thanks, honey." I was feeling a little better.

Suddenly Brian was James Bond again. "You can thank me in person tonight, you little vixen!"

"Brian—" But he had hung up, no doubt chuckling at unnerving me yet again. I wondered if I'd ever be romantic again without picturing Mavis Cunningham standing at the foot of our bed, gasping.

I called Mavis back and tried to gloss over the whole thing. "Brian is such a kidder," I said.

Her silence told me she wasn't buying it for a second, but she thoughtfully dropped the subject and we got back to business.

That evening at dinner, I could hardly eat. Brian snickered, knowing full well why I'd lost my appetite. "Lost in Andyland again?" he whispered.

I frowned. "Let's tell a story in a round," I suggested, trying to get my mind off the day's blunder. The kids all cheered, eager to twist my cotton candy fairy tales into the weird stories they love to concoct.

"Once upon a time there was a beautiful princess," I started.

Brian was next. "But she fell under the spell of the evil Vampira." He grinned. He loves to side with the kids in their efforts to monsterize everything.

"Vampira threw her in a big pot of boiling water," Erica said, thoroughly enjoying my disappointment.

"And then she ate her!" Grayson shouted, thrilled with this turn of events.

"Who ate whom?" Brian asked, so we paused to clarify that Vampira ate the princess.

Now it was Ryan's turn. He grinned. "And then she threw up the princess and it got all over everything."

This was not boosting my appetite and I rolled my eyes. "Good grief," I said, "who brought this up?"

"You did! You did!" the kids all cheered.

"Actually, I guess Vampira did," Brian said. Now the entire bunch exploded into fits of laughter, Grayson fell off his chair, Ryan inhaled some milk, and Erica began mopping tears of hysteria with the edge of the table-cloth.

I sighed and looked at Brian through narrow slits. "This is how they're going to act on their missions, you know."

Brian grinned. "That's okay. They always blame the mom."

I sat there, defeated, and wondered how to embroider an etiquette disclaimer onto the lapels of my sons' suits someday. "Their father is responsible," it would begin.

Finally the fireworks settled down and the kids returned to their dinner. I suppose I should have been glad that the whole thing didn't escalate into a food fight.

"Mom, how come there are roly-poly bugs on my chicken?" Ryan asked.

"Those are not sow bugs," I said. "They're capers."

"Tapeworms?" Grayson said, not having heard clearly.

"Capers," I said through my teeth.

Brian poked his around in the lemon sauce. "What are capers, anyway?" he asked.

"I don't know," I said, too weary to think about it.

"You mean you're feeding us things that you don't even know what they are?" Erica gasped. She was clearly making a mental list of traits she would not take into motherhood.

"It smells steamy in here," Grayson said.

"It's all the plants," I said. "It's like living in a green-house."

"I say we get rid of them," Brian said. "Nick and Zan will never know."

"Brian!" I nodded towards his listening offspring. "That wouldn't be the right thing to do." More nodding.

Brian looked at me. "Oh. You're talking *top* of the moral scale."

I sighed.

"I think these bushes are dangerous for the birds," Erica said, since the dutiful Wanda wasn't here to speak in behalf of the local wildlife. "They see all the leaves in here and then they fly into the windows."

"Yeah, and their families sit in the trees outside and watch," Ryan said, as if they were waving white hankies to their soldier sons on a steamer.

"They do kind of hover over the house," Brian said, glancing out the dining room window.

"Maybe they're hoping to catch a roly-poly bug," I muttered.

"Look at them lined up on the telephone wire," Ryan said, pointing with a piece of potato that he had speared with his fork.

"How come they're all bunched up on the two ends with a space between them?" Grayson asked.

"It's just like people," Brian said. "The group on the left is saying [now he spoke in a prissy little voice] you guys are disgusting—you just kill spiders for *sport!*"

I finally laughed for the first time all evening. I looked out the window at the birds and pictured Brian's feud. I glanced over at him, and he smiled. "Feeling better, yet?"

I smiled. "Some."

"Whose turn to clear the table?" Brian asked the kids.

"Not mine!" Grayson and Ryan said simultaneously, then, "Personal jinx."

I whispered to Brian, "I am so tired of this jinxing business when they say something at the same time." The rule was that the jinxer got to slug the jinxee if he spoke before his name was called so I quickly unjinxed them, "Grayson, Ryan."

Soon the kids were busy with their dish-washing chores, and Brian and I sat down in the living room. "Look at it this way," Brian said, knowing I still had Mavis Cunningham on my mind. "At least she knows we have a happy marriage. I mean, how often do you get a real peek behind closed doors? At least Mavis Cunningham knows that we're still crazy about each other."

"Or, just plain crazy."

"Hey," Brian said, "everyone knows you've been tee-tering on the brink of insanity for a long time."

I swatted him on the arm. "I have not!"

"Okay," he said. "You've been teetering on the brink of sanity, then."

I was too weak to punch him anymore and slumped against his shoulder. "Do you think I'll die of embarrassment someday?"

"It has to happen to somebody, sometime. I'd say you're a definite candidate."

"That was not the answer I was looking for."

Brian kissed me. "I know. But you don't want me to be predictable, do you?"

"Oh, don't worry," I said. Brian is the least predictable man I know, with the exception of Nick, who takes that virtue galloping straight into the realm of vice.

Just then Grayson came running into the living room, stunned and excited about something. "Hey, Mom!" he said, "you were right!!"

I looked up. "Thank-you for sounding so surprised. What was I right about?"

"That a leaf turns yellow if you clip a piece of black paper over it."

I smiled. Every time I know some simple piece of information, my kids go into shock. Now if only I could think of some experiment that would make this forest disappear.

"Mom," Ryan said, holding up a toy police car, "What is another name for this car?" Then he began making clicking noises with his tongue.

"What are you doing?" I asked.

"I'm timing you."

"Timing me?! What—we're on Jeopardy?"

"Tick-tock-tick-tock—"

"Stop that!" I said. "I will not be timed."

Ryan put a chubby little hand on his hip. "Do you know the answer?"

I fumed. "What do I win if I tell you?"

"Nothing."

"Fine. I don't know, anyway."

Ryan began rolling it away, across the back of a chair. "It's called a Wooka Noompa Gaga Car."

"Oh, well, everybody knows that," I muttered.

Brian hugged me. "Is this how your day goes when I'm not here?"

I smiled. "Sometimes Ryan gives me a little more time."

Soon Brother Laird showed up with the reception videotape, and Erica made some popcorn (for us to eat until the "surprise" made us lose our appetites again, I guess).

It started with the wedding ceremony, then cut to the reception while the photographer was taking pictures. Each one of us looked like a phony, grinning with elation for the photographer, then stepping aside with a long face after.

Brother Laird had interviewed several of the reception guests, many of whom shared their life's wisdom about how to make a marriage work.

"Congratulations," Elroy Morganstern grunted. "Just remember two words: Don't nag."

Next, one of Nick's practical joker buddies drummed up some genuine tears, talking about how emotional this was for him. "And I want to publicly apologize," he said, "for putting the snake in your luggage." Then he busted up laughing.

One of the clips showed Paula and Natalie stiffly expressing their "joy," which I found to be the funniest part yet.

Olive and Irving Archer offered some inspiring words, then Wanda said, "I've always felt that keeping a neat house is an important virtue." Brian and I shook our heads and smiled.

My mother was there, claiming to have always known Nick would settle down and be happy, then Edith Horvitz came on, twirling in that crocheted get-up.

Brian and I were on next, arms around each other, wishing Nick and Zan a great sense of humor and lots of pillow talk. My horrible permanent had grown out just enough to be pulled into a ponytail, but on tape it looked like a hedgehog had attached itself to the back of my neck.

Ryan made a cameo appearance at the children's table, stuffing handfuls of M&Ms into his mouth until Grayson yanked him out of the frame.

Erica showed up in the receiving line, shaking hands with a handsome deacon who was passing through. Naturally, we all took the opportunity to whistle and hoot.

The catering crew waved from their posts in the kitchen, Lara giggling as the videotape caught her nibbling on a canapé.

And of course the camera came back often to Nick and Zan, who were always dreamy-eyed and kissy, a real groaner for Ryan.

There was a wide shot of Edith trying to pawn off her tamales and of wary guests smiling but declining as they passed by.

Finally Brother Laird said, "Here comes the part I was telling you about." You mean refusing to tell me about, I thought.

The camera panned the elaborate feast on the buffet table, from one delectable end to the other. Suddenly we saw a hand reach into the frame and scoop an entire tray full of tiny sandwiches into a large purse.

We all gasped. The camera pulled back to reveal the culprit, Rita Delaney.

"Sister Delaney!" we all shouted together.

"Personal jinx, everyone," Grayson said.

"Stop with that jinxing," Brian said, leaping up to stand in front of the TV, just as we saw Rita glancing sideways to make sure no one was looking.

Brother Laird was holding his sides, laughing. "Isn't that the greatest?" he said. "Rita Delaney, that pinch-faced, old—" he stopped, taking note of our children.

"Well, you know how she's always telling everyone else what to do—"

"We cannot show this video to anyone else," Brian said.

Brother Laird was stunned. "But I've already sent it in!"

"Rita Delaney will never get over this," I gasped. "You've got to call the TV show and cancel the entry." I could just picture Rita having a heart attack when her footage was awarded ten thousand dollars.

"Oh, she already knows about it," Brother Laird says. "She said she wants to split the profits with me if it wins."

Brian was groping for words. "Wasn't she even a little embarrassed?"

"Until I told her how much she could win."

"But what about her reputation, her good name?" I said, sounding like an aproned mother in a Norman Rockwell painting.

Brian shrugged. "I guess everybody has a price."

"Well," I said, "Mine would be plastic surgery and a new residence out of state."

Brian smiled. "The Witness Protection Program again." Or, in this case, witless.

"That's right," I said. "How does she expect to live this down?"

"By living it up," Grayson said and grinned.

"Well, we can't stand by and let dishonesty go rewarded like that," I huffed, trying to wring a lesson out of this for my children. "I think she should... at least reimburse Nick and Zan for the cost of the sandwiches."

"She'd still net a profit," Erica said, sharing a brilliant piece of deduction from the economics unit she studied in school this year. "Let's see, five thousand dollars minus four bucks for the sandwiches ... "

I turned to Brian for some help. "We will definitely see that she pays the proper consequences," Brian said.

The kids stared at us. "How?" Grayson asked.

"Uh, we'll think about it," Brian said, clearly without one idea.

The kids began talking all at once about various punishments for Sister Delaney. Brian whispered to me, "You notice she didn't steal the tamales."

"Maybe we should all go over to her house and tell her we forgive her," I said.

Brian's face lit up. "Hey, that ought to awaken a lively sense of guilt."

I smiled. "And then we'll say that, as a token of our friendship, we'd like to give her a little gift."

Brian raised his eyebrows, clearly impressed with this plan and unaware that I was kidding.

"And she'll open it up," I said, "and it will be a great big, red and yellow macaw." I grinned. I figured it was the least we could do.

CHAPTER 9

PACKING IT IN

You know you need a vacation when you haven't used your luggage in so long that you can't remember where it's stored.

"I am not buying new suitcases," Brian growled.

I stood, sweating, amidst boxes of Christmas ornaments and bundles of my old term papers. "Brian, I have dragged every box and basket out of every corner of this house," I said. "Unless you can think of one more place where an entire set of luggage could be hiding, I'm going to the Hartman outlet with my VISA card."

Suddenly Brian's eyes lit up. "The attic!" he shouted and sprinted into the garage for the ladder.

"How come you guys waited until the day before our trip to get the luggage out?" Erica asked.

I sighed. Only yesterday the honeymooners came and hauled off the jungle of trees we'd been swatting aside, finally clearing the way to all our storage space. "We like excitement," I said.

Nick and Zan had returned from Africa with dozens of souvenirs and photographs. Their house was freshly painted, their wedding proofs were ready, their answering machine tape was full of information about who gave them which gifts, and now a crew of landscapers was eagerly transforming their dirt yard into a grassy park, burgeoning with trees and flowers.

"Marriage is wonderful," Zan purred.

So is access to your closets, I thought, appreciating how big our house looked now, without all the plants.

"I found them!" Brian's voice was muffled as he shouted from inside the attic. "Let me hand them down to you." I stood below the opening to the attic as Brian lowered the suitcases, then some cardboard boxes.

"What are these?" I asked.

"I don't know, but we ought to label them or throw them away," Brian said.

I carried the boxes into the bedroom and opened them on the bed. "My old baby clothes!" I said, eager to lift out the tiny, lace-trimmed gowns and frilly little slips. My mother presented me with this box of memorabilia when she moved into a smaller place, and having the same pack-rat genes as my mother, I had faithfully stored it away in the attic. Erica wandered in to appreciate the moment with me, but my smile faded as I saw how truly *old* everything looked. My teeny little satin shoes looked like some crackly, stiff museum offering, the sort you'd find near a wax replica of Betsy Ross. I can't possibly be that old, I thought to myself. In fact, *nobody* can be that old.

"Whose bonnet?" Erica asked, picking up a cap of feathery lace that hung like cobwebs from her fingers.

"Oh, just some leftover memorabilia they found with the Dead Sea Scrolls in the caves at Qumran," I said.

"You'd better pack for the trip and play antiques later," Brian said, walking in and dropping the largest bag down onto the bed. I gave him a look. "What—" he said. "What did I do now?"

I sighed, took one last look at my ancient wardrobe, then packed it up, a time capsule to be opened in another twenty years or so. "Will you put this back in the attic?" I asked Brian.

"Sure," he said scooping up the box, then pausing at the doorway. "And I wish you the best with your crippling arthritis."

I scowled. Okay, I could have put the box in the attic myself. But the reality of how long ago I wore those disintegrating clothes had suddenly made me feel feeble.

The kids began loading their essentials into suitcases. Ryan had already collected a pile of toys he wanted to take along, which would have required a cargo plane all its own if we had let him bring them. "You kids can take whatever you can fit into your own backpacks," I said, neatly stacking socks and underwear in the larger bags. "And what won't break your heart to lose." I had already loaded a Zip-Loc bag for each of them, filled with gimmicks to entertain them on the long flight: pipe cleaners, origami paper, stickers, puzzles, books and crayons. Grayson found my taste decidedly schoolish, and began loading his bag with rocks, squirt guns, and hideous little figurines of Saturday morning cartoon monsters who try to take over the world.

"Does it feel hot in here to you?" I asked Brian, slumping down onto the bed and fanning myself with a travel brochure.

Brian's face lit up, and he raised his fists in triumph. "Yes! Yes!"

"You're cheering that it's hot?" I asked.

Brian placed his hands on my shoulders. "No—You're finally having hot flashes. This is the day I've been waiting for!"

I swatted his bald head with the brochure. "All this time you've been waiting for menopause?"

Brian blinked. "Of course. Doesn't everybody?"

I closed my eyes. Surely there must be medication for Brian's brand of reasoning.

"Think about it," Brian said, "We won't have to worry about getting pregnant anymore! I'd say it's definitely something to look forward to. Although you are pretty young for it . . . "

"There isn't a man on this planet who sounds sensible discussing female hormones," I said.

Brian smiled. "On the other hand, you live in Southern California. You're probably just hot. Also, you've been unloading closets all morning. And, you're excited about the trip."

I nodded. Those were reasons enough to take a rest.

Brian sat beside me. "Or maybe you just want my body."

"That's it," I smiled. "I knew you'd come around to this."

Brian touched his nose to mine and ran his hand along my leg. "Just wait till . . . " he glanced toward the hallway where our children were noisily preparing for the trip. "Till . . . " then he frowned. "Till we get back, probably."

I laughed. "I love you," I said. "And I'd wait forever for you."

"Hey, Mom—" Ryan called from the hallway. "The air conditioner is making a funny sound."

Brian covered his ears with his hands. "Not one more repair," he said. "I can't take it."

"Come on," I laughed and pulled him to the hallway. Sure enough, the vent was buzzing its last breath. "So," I whispered to Brian. "My hot flashes turned out to be a broken air conditioner."

"Just what we need," he said. "Well, we can all sleep with the windows open tonight, and then we can get it fixed when we get home, I guess."

A few minutes later, Brian dashed into the bedroom out of breath. "Where's Gizmo?" This question signals an immediate halt to any and all activities, as we mobilize to hunt down a dog whose sole mission in life—after eating piano parts—is to escape into the wilds of suburbia. He will pretend to be napping, but will have one eye cracked open as people come and go, waiting for the rare opportunity to bolt through a door left carelessly ajar.

"Gizmo! Gizmo!" we all called at the top of our lungs in all corners of the house and yard.

"I guess he got out when I went to get the ladder," Brian said.

"We won't leave without him, will we?" Erica asked.

Brian paused just a second too long.

"Daddy! How could you?!" Erica looked as if she had caught him giggling over her diary.

"Erica, I—wait—" Brian called after her, to no avail. Erica had fled to her room in tears.

Brian turned to me. "I didn't say *anything*!"

"That seems to be the problem," I said.

Brian slumped into a chair. "This better not signal some adolescent stage that we have to endure for another four years."

"Eight."

"Sheesh!" Brian pulled himself out of the chair and went to Erica's room to try and convince her that he would gladly forgo a free trip to Europe to wait for Gizmo to come home with a belly full of garbage and a coat full of mud.

I turned to Grayson and Ryan. "He'll come home," I said, knowing full well that Gizmo always had before, but not always within 24 hours. "If worse comes to worse, maybe Grandma will come over and stay here to watch for him." My mother had offered to watch Gizmo while we were gone, and we'd planned to take him over to her house first thing in the morning.

Naturally, Erica refused to pack for a trip that she was convinced she would have to sacrifice as the lone member of our family who cared about *all* God's creations, not just the English countryside. Her plan was to keep a silent vigil, watching at the window for the Prodigal Dog.

"We all love Gizmo," I tried to explain to her that night.

"But you won't give up the trip for him."

"I might," I said, not wanting to commit. "Let's just see if he comes home first, and maybe everything will work out fine."

"But I'll always know what you really would have done."

I smiled and touched noses with her. "No," I said, "then you'll never know what any of us would have done."

She smiled. "I know you love him, too," she said. "I just worry when he gets out."

Wait until you have kids, I wanted to say. Someday you're going to get a driver's license and I'll need sedation just to tie my shoes. Someday some D-student with acne, a motorcycle, and a bad haircut will come and pick you up for a date.

You talk about worry. Not that I didn't worry about Gizmo, too. Wasn't I the one stapling "Lost Dog" fliers on the telephone poles during last year's freak blizzard while he was happily carrying on the romance of the year with a Labrador two blocks away? And didn't I fork out a hundred bucks to a company that claimed they could find him by calling every house in a radius around ours? I'd probably scrounge up ransom money if somebody kidnapped that lousy mutt. But keep the whole family home from Europe when my mom could sit and tap her foot as easily as I could? Probably not.

And then, as if the Good Luck Fairy finally changed her flight pattern and decided to shower the Taylor home with a few bits of magic dust, I heard Ryan screaming from the front porch, "He's home! He's home!"

We all ran to the front door as if this were a corny movie about some returning war hero. "I swear that dog just does this for the attention," I said to Brian. Sure enough, the kids were smothering him with kisses, and he was lapping it all up. Brian patted his head as Gizmo padded by, en route to his water dish. "Oh, ye of little brains," he said. Then to me, "I nearly canceled my ticket."

"What?! For that sneaky, shaggy, piano-eating—"

"No," Brian said. "For Erica."

"Oh, Daddy!" Suddenly Erica dashed in from the doorway where she had overheard how much her father loved her. "I just knew you really cared!" She dissolved into tears and kisses, all over Brian's cheeks. He blushed and I smiled.

Elated and eager to pack now, Erica hurried out of his arms toward the hall. But just before leaving, she turned and gave me a look of disgust. "Shaggy—humph!" Then she turned on her heels and left.

"Well, once again I have lost the Congeniality Award," I said. "Daddy can do no wrong, and Mom's in the doghouse again."

Brian laughed and kissed me. "Just think, by this time tomorrow, all this will be forgotten and we'll be on our way to London, then Paris . . . "

I smiled. This trip was exactly what I needed.

CHAPTER 10

THE CLAMPETTS GO
ON VACATION

The next morning we took Gizmo over to my mother's house. From the long look on his face, you'd think he somehow knew about the wheat germ she'd sprinkle on his dog food.

"Are you sure he'll get along with Caruso?" Erica asked. Caruso is the loudest tenor cat in the history of singing cats (a history unknown to people with regular cats, but vivid indeed to those who own singers). Caruso's sole purpose in life, after chasing mice and crickets, is to perch atop the neighbor's fence and sing until someone throws a rock in his direction, at which point he finishes the howling from his camouflage station in a camellia bush.

"They'll get along fine," Mother insisted.

"Oh, yes," I said. "Gizmo wouldn't hurt a fly." Indeed, Gizmo had already hopped up onto a sofa cushion, turned his customary two circles, and plopped down as if he owned the place, glancing with only half interest in Caruso's direction.

Caruso seemed even less concerned than Gizmo. Instead, he focused on a bit of thread two feet away and crouched, staring.

"Look—he's going to pounce," Ryan said.

Then, as all people do when a cat begins playing, we fell silent and watched to see what Caruso would do next. He adjusted his feet. He arched his back. He paused, and then—he threw up.

"Oh, my gracious," Mother said and darted into the kitchen for some paper towels.

"Yuck!" my children said, with Erica adding, "Disgusting."

"Well, I'm certainly glad we all gathered round to watch that," Brian said.

"Maybe we shouldn't leave Gizmo," I said, carrying the cat into the laundry room. "Obviously it's upsetting Caruso."

"Oh, nonsense," Mother called to me. "He'll adjust."

"Well, I feel guilty leaving you with this," I said.

"Don't be silly," Mother said. "Have a good time. If he starts to lose weight, I'll just take him to the vet, that's all."

Now I *really* felt guilty. "Oh, Mom—I feel like we're really doing something terrible here—"

"What's to feel terrible about? You're going to Europe. I've heard it's wonderful."

At this point I reached Guilt Overload and Brian cleared his throat. "Let's thank Grandma again, kids," he said, steering me by the shoulders back to the car. Then he leaned in to my ear and whispered, "Glad she didn't go the guilt route."

"But I feel so bad that she's never been to Europe," I whispered back.

"Even though she disowned Nick and has only herself to blame," Brian said.

"Then why do I feel so responsible?" I asked him.

"Because your mother wrote the book on inducing guilt. Face it, Andy, you're in the hands of a master."

I smiled, and the kids came walking out to the car wearing confused expressions. I glanced back at my mother on the porch and saw why. She was leaning weakly against the doorway, saying, "Don't worry about me being here all by myself. I'll be fine."

"Shall we really leave Grandma?" Ryan asked, clearly swallowing her entire act.

"Absolutely," Brian said (a little too cheerily, perhaps). "She and Gizmo will be just fine. She said so herself."

No wonder Nick was so convincing all those years; he'd inherited his acting skills from Mom.

At last we pulled up at Nick and Zan's, and within a minute, Robbins, their driver, was there to take us to the airport.

"That's what I like," Nick said. "Perfect timing."

"You mean close calls," Brian said. "We nearly had to leave Andy at your mother's to take care of the animals."

Nick smiled. "I'm sure there won't be any more robberies on that block."

"What?!" I gasped.

Nick threw his head back and burst into laughter. "Works every time."

I set my jaw and we all piled into the roomy limo.

"Are you sure you're going with us?" Brian asked me one last time.

I'd been waffling lately, worried about all the people in the ward who were having babies, surgeries, and funerals. My counselors kept assuring me that they'd take care of everything—and besides, there is no window of calm in a ward of five hundred people; if you wait for that you'd never get a vacation. But I still felt like I was abandoning ship. "I am absolutely, positively going," I said to Brian, patting his leg. "Yep, almost definitely." Brian laughed.

Within no time, we were making no time. Why does every trip to the airport have to include a monumental tie-up on the freeway?

"There's California's state bird," Brian said, pointing at the cars that were creeping slowly around another stalled one. "The famous rubber-necked gawker." (I personally think the traffic is slowed by power fiends who race ahead, then deliberately slow down, waiting to hear about themselves on the radio traffic reports.)

"You sure you kids still want to go to Europe?" Nick asked. "You know tonight's the big meteor shower."

"Meat-eater shower?" Grayson asked, incredulous.

"Right," Brian said. "Huge tyrannosaurs fall from the sky and eat up all the plant-eaters."

Grayson smirked. "Da-ad."

Now Erica became giggly at the thought of meat-eaters falling from the sky, and Ryan began impersonating every dinosaur he could think of, including some I cannot hope to pronounce.

"There really is a falling star show every August," Nick went on.

"This doesn't have anything to do with the Emmy Awards," Brian said to the kids.

"They can pummel the landscape," I said, "as long as they don't fall on our airplane."

The kids began bouncing on the seats and cheering about going to Europe, springing into the air as they'd say, "Yur-UP!"

"Settle down, kids," Brian and I said simultaneously.

"You two will be talking in tandem, soon," Brian said to Nick and Zan.

"Jinx, Mom and Dad!" Grayson shouted.

"No more jinxing!" Brian and I said, together again.

Zan began laughing. "Is this going to last throughout the trip?"

Ryan kept flipping the switches at his armrest and Erica was opening and closing the beverage compartment. "Stop fiddling, you kids." Brian's eyes were turning into little x's. "Grayson, be quiet. Everyone calm down."

"They're excited," I apologized to Nick and Zan.

"I am not going to lose my temper," Brian vowed through his teeth.

I beamed. "Wonderful!"

"Oh—like it's a news bulletin," he said.

Grayson caught a glimpse of a sign out the window as he was bouncing in his seat. "Daddy, what's a swap meet?"

Brian sighed. "It's where people take their children . . . "

"Brian!" I said.

"... who've been particularly disruptive..." Brian continued.

Zan was looking out the window, too. "I drove this road for six years," she said.

"Whoa," Ryan said. "That's a long time to be lost, Aunt Zan."

Now we all burst out laughing, then Brian held up a dollar bill. "Whose dollar?"

"Mine, mine!" all three children screamed.

"Not an honest one in the bunch," Brian said. "If you kids can't keep track of your money, let Mom or me carry it."

"I can, I can!" they all yelled.

"It will seem quieter once we're in the airport," I said to Nick and Zan. They smiled.

Then Erica, Grayson, and Ryan began asking questions as quickly and loudly as they could, alternately whining that the others were interrupting them. "Plus Ryan is pushing me," Erica said.

"I am not."

"No he isn't," Grayson said, siding with his brother.

"You stay out of this," Erica said to Grayson.

By the time we arrived at the airport, every adult in the car—including Robbins—was ready for a mental evaluation. Our patience had been stretched to the snapping point, and it was all Brian or I could do to growl through our teeth, "Settle down, you kids!" Obviously, we had not taken enough vacations, nor enough tranquilizers.

In the elevator, Grayson pulled his shoe off and taped it to his back with a gummy length of tape he'd found on the floor. He announced that this would keep him from snoring on the airplane because he would be unable to roll onto his back.

"Put your shoe on," I said.

Grayson then unzipped Ryan's backpack, removed a toy car, and said he knew how to blow on it to make it sound like a kazoo.

Ryan snatched it back, shoved it into his own mouth, and began inhaling.

"You sound like a seal," Grayson told him. Then he began barking along to show Ryan how he sounded.

"No. This is how you do it," Ryan instructed, sucking in again.

Erica, unable to contain her excitement—and having just learned something new in ballet class—began doing pirouettes, bouncing up and down and shaking the elevator car.

When the doors opened, Nick and Zan bolted out, followed by Brian, who mumbled, "I'm going to Europe with one child who has a shoe taped to his back and who is barking like a seal, another child who is bouncing like a ping pong ball, and another who is demonstrating how to suck cars."

I sighed and bodily pulled the children from the elevator.

At the security X-ray gates, a uniformed guard unzipped Grayson's backpack and, shaking a stern finger, removed a set of plastic nunchakus.

"Hey," Brian said to Nick and Zan, "We should have brought your wedding gifts here to be X-rayed, then you could just keep the good stuff."

As soon as we gathered our carryons again, we checked the monitor to see if the flight was still on schedule.

"Uh-oh," Nick said, "we're delayed over an hour." Then he spotted a café. "Shall we have a little snack while we wait?"

The kids all cheered and I cringed. I should have packed a change of clothes for each of them in my purse.

On the way to the restaurant, Brian stopped at a replica of Los Angeles in a glass case. "It's so hard to go home again," he said wistfully. "Everything always looks so much smaller." I rolled my eyes and pulled him along.

In the restaurant Nick said he was keeping our hotel a secret and mentioned that he and Zan would be staying with a dear friend of his. "But you'll love your hotel," he said. "It's fabulous. And in two nights, I'd like you to come to a big fireside. A friend of mine is the mission president, and he asked me to give a speech to the missionaries."

"Oh, wonderful, Nick!" I said. "He couldn't have picked a better speaker." Nick was still as smooth as ever, only now his talents could be used to motivate and inspire, instead of to keep himself undercover.

The waitress took our orders, then the kids began talking about their hero, Uncle Nick. "He is so brave it's awesome," Grayson said.

"Hey," Brian said, "I believe *I* am the one ordering the tuna sandwich. That kind of bravery is in a class by itself."

"Yes," I said. "The name of the category is 'foolhardy.'"

"I have a theory," Brian said, ignoring me. "I think the French invented croissants to make the whole rest of the world look like slobs. Those things shower crumbs everywhere. Also, they knew no one would be able to pronounce it."

"Look," I said, pointing at the vast array of nationalities represented in the families at the café. "Here's your chance to learn, 'Don't blow bubbles with your straw,' in seven different languages."

Grayson's french fries arrived, sizzling and golden. One by one, we all began snitching a fry here and there, until Grayson—who always scored high on problem-solving—abruptly spat onto his plate.

"Oh, gross!" Erica howled.

I stared at the string of spit that lay defiantly across the fries.

"You are truly disgusting," I said.

"Thank-you." Grayson grinned and happily chomped his suddenly unpopular fries.

As I finished off the scrambled eggs I'd ordered, I noticed Brian smirking at them. "You have a problem with my eggs?" I smirked right back at him.

He shook his head. "Such a wimpy way to eat eggs. Eggs should be fried, over easy. Period."

"Oh, right," I said. "So the raw yolk can run all over the plate like radioactive ooze."

"Hey," Brian said. "If God had intended eggs to be scrambled, then chickens would walk like this." He then got up and demonstrated a chicken, arms flailing in all directions and shaking from head to foot as he strutted down the aisle.

"They do," I said. "They peck and go like this." I then got up and demonstrated how chickens *do* bob their heads back and forth, flapping my arms to indicate further natural scrambling.

"They do not," Brian argued. "They jive. They kind of glide, like this." He then changed his demonstration to look like a chicken on "Soul Train."

"Like this." I said, reprising my staccato pecking dance.

"Like this," Brian said, adding a new wing motion to his rendition. Vacation excitement had not only zinged our children with hyperactivity, it had also driven Brian and me over the edge. Everyone but Erica was laughing.

"Uncle Nick," Ryan said, "you know all about chickens. Why don't you show them the right way to do it?"

Nick smiled. "Not for a million dollars."

Erica was turning deep shades of crimson and glancing around for other adolescents she might possibly know. "Uncle Nick, can't we leave them home?" she asked.

"Erica, if there were enough people to make a crowd, they would make one in a circle around your parents, right now," he replied.

I glanced back and saw Erica on the verge of hysterical embarrassment. I turned to Brian. "Fine, you win the chicken award," I said.

Brian straightened his collar and smoothed his hair. "I should hope so," he huffed.

When it was finally time to board, Erica walked briskly ahead, pulling Zan along with her. Clearly, she was hoping that she and Zan looked like mother and daughter, while I was the lucky housekeeper who got to tag along this time.

"Just for the record," I whispered to Brian as we headed to the gate, "if God had wanted people to eat eggs over easy, then chickens would do flips as they're walking along. Like cheerleaders."

"Tumbling chickens."

"That's right," I said. "And I'd demonstrate, but I don't want to embarrass Erica any further."

"Ah." Brian shook his head. "My wife, the closet gymnast."

I pressed my face into Brian's and grinned. "There are lots of things you don't know about me, buddy boy."

"All as surprising as mid-air somersaults, I'm sure."

Our seats were in the section behind Nick's and Zan's; we figured we could at least give the newlyweds *some* privacy.

Finally, the kids worked out a sharing arrangement for the window seat, crammed their backpacks under the seats in front of them, and buckled up.

Brian and I settled in across the aisle from the children and closed our eyes.

"Uh-oh," I said, my eyes suddenly wide open and my throat tingling. "Oh, my heavens. I think I'm going to be sick," I said.

"Don't worry about the movie," Brian said, his eyes still closed. "They edit the flight films—"

"Hold my purse!" I said, shoving my bag into Brian's lap and bolting for the rest room. Other passengers were trying to find their seats, but I barreled through the huddle like a star fullback.

"What is Mom doing now?" I could hear Erica ask in more embarrassed tones.

I felt bad to knock everybody over in my mad dash, but I think the alternative would have been worse. After what seemed like an eternity in a metal closet, I made my way weakly back to my seat.

"Are you okay?" Brian asked.

I took my purse. "I've got to get some Dramamine or something," I said. "I'll be right back."

"You can't leave!" Brian said.

"I can't fly all the way to England without something," I whispered. "They aren't going to leave for twenty minutes and I'll be right back."

"How can you be sick?" Brian called after me. "The plane isn't even moving!"

I hurried back into the airport and searched for a gift shop. Just as I saw one, I felt horribly ill again and darted into a ladies' room. This time I barely made it into a stall.

After several minutes, I could hear another woman at the sinks, saying, "That woman must have food poisoning."

The eggs—could I have salmonella poisoning? Are all comedians right and airport food can really kill you? I couldn't believe how violently ill I felt. Or, maybe it was the flu, I thought. What a terrible way to start a vacation! And what if I gave the flu to everyone else?

Self-hypnosis, I thought to myself. Just tell yourself you feel better, clean up and go back to the plane. But no matter how I tried to convince myself, there was no way I could stop.

Suddenly, they were announcing the last call for boarding and there wasn't a single thing I could do, but crouch over a toilet and cry. Then I realized that everything would be fine; Brian would explain the situation and have them hold the plane. Just relax, I told myself. Get better.

When I finally felt able to walk out of the rest room, I quickly bought some motion sickness pills and hurried to the gate.

"I'm the one you've been holding the plane for," I explained to a uniformed woman behind the counter. "I'm terribly sorry."

"Which plane is that?" the woman asked.

"The flight to London," I said.

Now the woman looked out the window where the jumbo jet used to be, then back at me again. "It left ten minutes ago."

"What?! But that's impossible! I'm on that flight!"

The woman smiled. "Not unless you're a hologram, honey."

I couldn't believe this was happening. "My family is on that plane!"

"If you have your ticket, I can try to book you on the next available flight."

"It's on the airplane," I tried to explain. "But my name is Andy Butler. I mean Andy Taylor. But the tickets are under Nick Butler."

The woman stared over her glasses at me. "Would you like to sit down for a few minutes and decide who you are, then come back?" People were crowding behind me, anxious about making their own flights.

"I do not need to sit down," I said, trying to control myself. "Please book me on the next flight to London."

She tapped my request into a computer and found me a seat on another airline, leaving in two hours. I arranged for Brian to receive a message when they landed that I'd be two hours behind them.

After the longest two hours of my life (next to labor time) I had finally found the other airline gate, got my ticket squared away, and was just ready to board, when a voice over the intercom said, "Attention, all airline personnel and passengers. All further flights are cancelled. Attention. All flights are cancelled."

CHAPTER 11

LITTLE ORPHAN ANDY

A huge roar arose from the confused passengers as the clerks answered ringing phones. "What does that mean?" I asked. "What's going on?"

My new clerk hung up his phone. "Pilots' strike," he said. He then listed the airlines affected by the strike. I couldn't believe this was happening.

Passengers clamored for the only seats available on other airlines, and within minutes every alternate flight was booked for two days.

"We'll call you in a couple of days, as soon as we can find you a seat," he said to me.

"What about the flight to London that left two hours ago—will they come back?" I asked.

"Nope," the man said. "It's a nonstop. They'll continue on to London."

"Is there some way—" My question was buried under a crush of shoving passengers waving tickets, demanding refunds, yelling about luggage, and storming in circles around me.

Finally, I pushed back through the crowd and convinced the man that this was an emergency and I had to speak with my husband on the airplane. He called internal communications, who typed the jet's code into a computer and sent a message to the pilot on a video screen. The pilot then summoned a flight attendant, who announced to the entire plane, "Mr. Brian Taylor, please identify yourself. We have a message from your wife who you left at the airport in Los Angeles." (I later heard that the entire planeload of passengers erupted into laughter and that Brian had blushed down to his shoelaces.) From a telephone on the plane, Brian dialed me at the pay phone where I was waiting.

"Well," Brian drawled into the phone, "this one I gotta hear."

"Hey, it's not like I planned this!"

"Mmm-hmm."

"And how about you?" I shouted. "You didn't even miss me! Why didn't you ask them to hold the plane?"

"Hey—I did ask. Finally a flight attendant said the rest of the party was seated up front. I figured you sat down with Nick and Zan for the takeoff, to be closer to the rest room. Obviously, the flight attendant must have thought you were Zan. Then when I went to check on you, I figured you were kneeling at the throne again. What on earth happened to you?"

"I was so sick I couldn't get back in time."

"See, Andy, the way it works is, the people in the air get motion sickness. The people on the ground feel fine."

"Oh, stop it. I must have the flu or food poisoning or something."

Now I could hear Brian talking to the children, who had followed him to the phone. "Hey, kids—your mother really is back in Los Angeles. She missed the flight!"

I could only imagine Erica's embarrassed reaction.

Brian was back on the phone again. "This is all a plot to stick me with three kids who are so wired they set off the metal detectors, isn't it?"

I sighed.

Brian continued. "Actually, it's that you're suspicious of any country where the people run around saying 'wee wee,' isn't it?"

It's useless to interrupt Brian when he's on a roll.

"Wait a second," he went on. "Did some Ninja pigs have anything to do with this?"

"Your jokes are costing us nine dollars a minute, Brian. Come on—I'm stranded here."

"Stranded? I don't think so. You have all the com-
forts of home. We're the ones left stranded up in the
sky with no mother." (And he thinks my mom is the
master guilt-inducer.) "You said you'd follow me to the
ends of the earth," Brian went on. "Ha!"

"Actually, I once pointed out that you were dragging me to the ends of the earth," I said. "Be serious.
What should I do?"

I could hear the kids in the background now, clamor-
ing to find out how I bungled this one. "Mommy is feeling sick," Brian explained to them.

Then I could hear Ryan, whose volume knob broke
off in the delivery room, shouting, "She probably upset
her stomach walking like a chicken."

And Brian agreed with him! Then Brian spoke into
the phone again. "Don't worry, Babe. Just take the next
flight. We'll meet you at the airport."

"I can't. There's a pilots' strike."

"What?! You've got to be kidding. Boy, talk about
Vacatious Disruptus."

Now I could hear Brian explaining the pilots' strike
to Nick, and Nick saying, "That can't last long. Tell her
to hang tight." I pictured him giving this kind of advice
on a walkie-talkie to some fellow spy being shot at in an
alley.

"Hang tight," Brian said. "I'll call you at home when
we land and see if you've been able to book a flight out."

"I guess that's all we can do. Thanks, honey."

"Hey, no problem. After all, I exist ... to make you
happy."

"You're such a pal."

"I do love you, Andy. Feel better."

"I love you, too."

With that, I caught a shuttle bus to take me back to
an empty house. As we bounced along I caught a
glimpse of myself in the outside rearview mirror. Hmm,
I thought, objects in this mirror are stupider than they
appear. How could this have happened to me? This

whole thing was unbelievable, unfunny, unfair—pick an un. Any un.

I looked in the mirror again at my bedraggled reflection. Despite looking like a bag lady, at least I was feeling better. Whatever had upset my stomach seemed to be gone, now.

As the bus pulled away and I walked to my front door, I suddenly realized I had no house key. I had left all my keys home in another purse since I wouldn't be needing them on the trip. *Well, this is just great.* I circled the house trying every door and window, but everything was locked tight.

Then I remembered the doggie door. Of course—that was the perfect solution. I darted around the back of the house and up the back steps. Reaching through the rubber flap, I felt my way up the door for the lock. Nothing. I angled my shoulder through the opening and reached as high as I could, but I was still low by several inches. Finally, I thought I'd just stick my head and both shoulders in, maybe then—

Suddenly, the phone started ringing. The airline! It had to be them calling. I decided to just climb all the way through and make it to the phone before the machine picked it up.

One last push—uh oh. I was in serious trouble. I had pulled myself halfway into the kitchen and now I couldn't get in or out. I looked like Winnie the Pooh stuck in a knothole.

The phone kept ringing and I kept pushing, but I was wedged in as tight as a cork. Finally I heard the answering machine, then Claudia Lambert's voice. "Hi. I just thought I'd let you know everything's going fine with the pig," she said. "Oh—and we named him Curly."

Good grief—they named that luau pig Curly. Suddenly the phone was ringing again, and I pushed harder, trying to get in to answer it. The machine picked up again, and this time it was Edith Horvitz. "Hi, Andy. I've got a great idea for homemaking night." I closed my eyes. Edith went on. "House Make-overs." Oh, help us. Edith's cheery voice continued. "I'll take pictures of some of the sisters' homes, then we'll get a garden expert from the nursery to redesign everybody's landscape. I already talked to the guy, and he's willing to do it for free, figuring some people will take his advice and buy some plants there."

Not more plants—if I see another bush or tree . . .

"Oh, by the way," Edith said, "have you left on your trip, yet?" (How could I respond if I had?) "Well, bye!"

I slumped onto the floor, the sharp edge of the doggie door pressing into my stomach. The house seemed unusually hot again, and I remembered the air conditioner was broken. I could see the headlines: Half Dog, Half Woman Found Dead of Heat Exhaustion.

Suddenly, I heard the doorbell ring. Someone was at the front door! "Help!" I called. "Help! I'm around back!"

"Is someone home?" I heard a man's voice call through the front door.

"Yes—around back!" I yelled, using what was left of my dissected diaphragm. Soon I heard footsteps behind me, but I couldn't see who was there. "Who is it?" I asked.

"Are you breaking in?" a man's voice asked.

Oh, don't tell me I'm being mistaken for a burglar again! "No," I said. "I live here, I'm just . . . stuck."

Now one man on my right began pushing me into the house, and another man on my left began pulling me out. "Wait," I called. "Which way are we going?"

Simultaneously one man said "in" as the other said "out."

"I think we'd better go in," I said. Then they both began pushing until my bottom fell onto the kitchen floor with a loud thunk! I was too grateful to be alive to be embarrassed. I pulled in my legs, stood up, and opened the door.

"Thank-you so much," I said, wiping sweat from my face. "This is all so embarrassing. I locked myself out."

The men smiled. I must have looked like I'd just crawled through a drain pipe.

"Hi, I'm Kirk Emery," the taller one said. He had thick lips and a spray of nutmeg-colored freckles across his cheeks. "And this is Stony Melendez." Stony was dark-skinned with a black mustache and wore his hair slicked back with comb lines running through it.

"Andy Taylor," I said and shook their hands.

"We're looking for Nick Butler."

"Oh—that's my brother. But you just missed him," I said. "He's on his way to England."

The men frowned. "Didn't he just get back from his honeymoon?"

"Oh, yes. But he's on his way to England, now. Are you friends of his?"

Kirk and Stony pulled out their wallets and showed me their CIA identification. "We were," Kirk said. "We . . . we need your help, ma'am."

"Why? What's wrong?" I invited the men in, apologized for the heat, and sat them at the kitchen table.

"Nick is . . . " Kirk was clearly uneasy. "We know he's your brother, so this is very hard to say. But there's some real danger involved here and we have to be honest with you."

"What—what is it?"

"Nick is an imposter, Mrs. Taylor."

CHAPTER 12

THE GRAND DECEPTION

I smiled at my visitors. "Oh—I know all about Nick's work for the government. He finally told us the truth."

Kirk and Stony exchanged glances. "Not exactly." They then went on to explain that Nick had indeed been working for the CIA, but had been fired years ago for some unscrupulous dealings.

"What?! That's impossible!" I said.

"Don't you think Nick seems a little wealthy for an intelligence agent?" Stony said.

I gulped. This couldn't be true—had Nick really lied to us yet again, saying he was retiring? I told them about Nick's helicopter landing and the letter from the President, thanking Nick for his years of service.

The men just smiled and shook their heads. "It would be nothing for Nick to arrange such a show in order to fool you," Stony said. "The truth is that Nick has been swindling and conning for years now, using many of the contacts he made in the agency. He was smart enough to get away with it for a while, but now he's in over his head."

I started to cry. My baby brother! "What has he done?"

Kirk and Stony stood up. "Excuse us for just one minute," Kirk said, then he and Stony stepped into the hall and whispered to each other.

My mind was racing a mile a minute. How could this be—was Nick's limo and extravagance the result of illegal dealings? What about Brian and the kids—alone

with him in another country? But then, what about his
marriage to Zan and how sincere Nick seemed about the
church?

I was at a complete loss. For years Nick had been
fooling me while my mother and sisters kept telling me
how gullible I was. Maybe they were right all along, and
I had swallowed yet another whopper. What kind of
danger had I put my own family in?

Kirk and Stony came back and sat down. "It's a very
serious matter, Mrs. Taylor. The agency believes Nick is
involved in an assassination plot."

The next thing I knew, Kirk was sponging my head
with a damp cloth, and I was lying on the kitchen floor,
coming to.

"I think she's going to be all right," Kirk was saying.
"You fainted, Mrs. Taylor."

"Nick would never kill anyone," I whispered, still
weak. I may have fallen for a lot of bunk in my time, but
I would never believe that Nick could commit a murder.

Kirk looked pretty shaken, too. "Mrs. Taylor, I was a
friend of Nick's a long time ago. I took it pretty hard
when he changed. I saw him do a lot of things that . . . I
just never thought he would."

"Money is a funny thing," Stony added. "People lose
perspective sometimes."

"But I can't believe that Nick would get involved
in . . . in something like that," I said.

Kirk and Stony just sat there, silent.

"Who is it?" I asked.

"The queen of England," Kirk said. "That's why we
were so . . . upset to hear he had already left."

I felt dizzy and sick again. "The queen of England?!
But why?"

"Mrs. Taylor, do you remember Nick traveling to
Central America?"

"Oh, many times."

"Did he ever mention the name Francisco Montoya?"

"No."

"He's one of the biggest drug lords in the world, and Nick works for him. Montoya wants to eliminate anybody who stands in his way."

"But—the queen of England?"

"She has more power than you think. She's calling for a lot of trade restrictions, and certain covert activities that Francisco Montoya doesn't like."

It was all I could do to stop shaking. How could my own brother get involved in something so devastating? "My husband and children are with him," I said. "We've got to call the police."

"Police are already involved," Kirk said. "We're working with them all the way."

"But... we've got to do something. Please promise me Nick won't be hurt. What about the safety of my husband and children?"

Kirk put a hand on my shoulder. "We don't want anyone to get hurt, ma'am. That's why we're going to try to apprehend him before it's too late."

"Can you tell us where he'll be staying?" Stony asked.

I tried to swallow but my throat was dry. "This can't be happening," I mumbled. "Not Nick..."

"Please, Mrs. Taylor," Stony said. "You have to help us."

"I...I don't know where they'll be," I said. "Nick was keeping the hotel a surprise, and he and Zan were going to stay with a friend. But my husband is going to call as soon as they land—"

"We can't let your husband or your children know about this," Kirk said.

"Why not?"

Kirk leaned in, dead serious. "This requires the utmost security, Mrs. Taylor. If anyone in your family should act suspicious or ask questions, Nick would sense trouble immediately. You're going to have to trust us to handle this. It's what we've been trained to do. You must not tell your husband until after we apprehend Nick."

I was still shaking, trying to listen, trying to grasp the seriousness of the situation. "Wait—I do know one place where he'll be, but it's in two nights. Will that be too late?"

"We think they've planned the hit for when the queen leaves for Scotland in five days."

"He's speaking at a fireside," I said.

"A what?"

"It's a big church meeting," I said. "But can't someone else intervene, who's already in England?"

"Not in this situation," Kirk said. "He needs to see me; he trusts me. If police simply grab him at the airport, Nick won't lead us to the others. I have to get over there and gain his trust."

"Wait a minute," I said. "Nobody can get over there. There's a pilot's strike and no flights are taking off."

Kirk and Stony didn't seem concerned. "Mrs. Taylor, air transportation is the least of our problems. We can use an agency plane."

"Take me with you!" I said. "I can't let you go and take my brother away without—I have to at least tell him good-bye. And I have to see my family. They're in danger."

Kirk and Stony shook their heads. "We simply can't do that," Kirk said. "You're really better off here, and it would be impossible to get special clearance under the circumstan—"

"I can take you to the fireside," I said. "You won't know how to get in unless you bring me with you."

"I'm sorry," Kirk said, as he and Stony stood to leave. "It would jeopardize the operation."

I had to think of a way to get them to take me along. "Well, you don't know my husband," I explained. "He can be trusted one hundred percent, and when he calls I'm going to tell him everything. I cannot let my family walk into some kind of a trap—"

Kirk glanced at Stony. "She'll blow it," he said. Stony nodded. Then Kirk turned to me. "You don't leave us much choice. Can you leave immediately?" he asked.

I never packed so fast in my life. I just grabbed bare essentials and threw them into an overnight bag. My

mind was spinning in agony, trying to remain calm and
think how to rescue my family while these men were
trying to capture Nick. Maybe if Nick could lead them to
others, then Nick would get a lighter sentence somehow.

"You're not going to hurt Nick, are you?" I asked as
I came back into the kitchen.

"No, ma'am. We need him. But you'll have to cooper-
ate fully on this trip and follow our directions. This is a
sting operation that's been planned for months. We're
taking our orders from Washington."

My heart was simply breaking, thinking of the trouble Nick was in. I was certain things couldn't get worse.

Enter Edith Horvitz. Just as we came around the
front of the house, there was Edith with her camera,
snapping a picture of us.

"Hey—who's that?" Kirk said.

"Oh, it's just Edith," I said. Edith was squatting down
on the front lawn getting a wide shot of the house. "Oh,
yeah," she was saying, taking pictures of the overgrown
bushes and trees in the yard.

"Edith—" I called.

She turned and snapped another picture of me with
the CIA agents.

"Don't tell her," Stony warned me. I trembled.

"Hey, Andy—you sure could use a make-over!" Edith's
tact is second only to her timing.

"Excuse me, ma'am, I have to ask for your camera,"
Kirk said, stepping forward and reaching for Edith's
Sure-Shot.

Edith pulled back. "Don't be so paranoid," Edith
said (a line she must have practiced for years in the
mental hospital). "It's only a front lawn!"

"Give me the camera," Kirk said.

"No way," Edith said, and then, as if this piece of
news should settle the matter, "This is for Homemaking
Night."

Kirk looked back at me. "What's that?"

"It's . . . it's a night," I fumbled, "when the women in
our church get together and do . . . well, several things.

Sometimes it's a lecture, or a community project, crafts—"

"We need the camera, ma'am," Stony told her, stepping up to join Kirk.

"Hey, Andy," Edith said, "Are these guys friends of yours?"

"Uh, I guess I should introduce you," I stammered. "This is Edith Horvitz. And these men . . . these men . . . "

"We're Kirk Emery and Stony Melendez," Kirk said. "You don't seem to realize who you're dealing with. We're from airport security. Mrs. Taylor missed her flight and we're going to see that she joins her family in England. However, we cannot be photographed on the job, so we'll have to take the film."

My mouth hung open. Until now, Nick was the only person I knew who could think that fast. But it evidently ran in the spy business.

Edith chortled. "And *you* don't seem to realize who *you're* dealing with. I'm the homemaking leader, and you're not getting this film." Edith has never underestimated the importance of her calling.

"We're prepared to pay for the film," Stony said.

Edith looked insulted. "I am on church business," she said. "How dare you try to tempt me not to do my job? Get me behind there, Satan."

I cringed. Why did Edith have to come by just now and snap their pictures?

"Would two hundred dollars cover it?" Kirk asked.

Edith folded her arms over the camera straps. "I wouldn't give you this film for a million bucks."

Kirk and Stony were stammering now. Obviously, they had never tried to negotiate with a slightly crazy, obsessed homemaking leader before.

"Look here, ma'am," Kirk said. "Either you give us that camera, or you'll have to come with us to England!"

Edith's eyes lit up. "Well, hot dawg! You got yourself a deal!"

"What?!" I exclaimed. "But she can't go—"

Edith was already getting her purse out of her car, as the agents tried to grasp what had just happened.

"She can't be serious," Kirk whispered.

"Oh, yes she can," I whispered back. "Edith's a little crazy—can't you tell? She thinks she's coming with us!"

"We can't risk having her develop that film while we're gone," Stony said to Kirk. "And we can't just yank the camera off her neck. Maybe this is actually safer."

I couldn't believe they were really considering it. Suddenly Edith was coming back up the driveway carrying a trash bag and a bird cage.

"Oh, no!" I said. "Not that macaw!"

"This is a choice?" Edith said, happily loading the bird cage into the car. "Give them my camera or get a free trip to England! And people think *I'm* nuts!"

"Edith," I said, "Don't you have to make arrangements? I mean, lock your apartment, or let people know you'll be gone, or . . . "

"Nope," Edith said. "I don't take the paper and my only pets are crocheted."

"What?" Stony asked.

"Don't ask," I whispered. "Edith, I don't think you can bring a bird on an airplane."

She laughed. "How do you think it got here from South America—flew to a pet shop?"

I turned to the agents. "She can't bring that bird, can she?"

"I can't leave it here," Edith interrupted. "It's me, the camera, and the bird, or nothing."

Kirk and Stony looked absolutely baffled by this bizarre predicament. "I suppose," Stony said.

I was groping for any reason why Edith had to stay here. "But she doesn't have a passport," I said.

Kirk stared at Edith with her nearly bald head, her turquoise eye shadow, and her yellow housecoat. He sounded almost reluctant to disagree with me, then said, "We've got plenty of passports."

I was out of ideas now, and watched grimly as Edith climbed into the backseat. "Didn't you take it to the zoo?" I asked.

"Yep. I was almost out the door, too," Edith said. "Then the bird started yappin', and they told me the zoo is a family place and, well, you've heard him."

I sighed and slumped down in the backseat, on the other side of the cage.

"Actually, I've grown kinda attached to him," Edith went on. "His name's Angel."

Angel?! Was she nuts? Well, okay, yes, Edith was nuts. But naming that creature Angel? Destroying Angel, maybe.

"What's in the trash bag?" I asked her.

"Oh—I didn't realize you were leaving today, and I was going to give this to Brian," Edith said. "But since we'll be seeing him in England, I thought I'd give it to him there. It's my new invention."

I remembered her particle board house and wondered what could possibly be her next extravaganza.

"It's the special glue I invented," Edith said. "It's even stronger than Crazy Glue. I want Brian to try it with a toupee."

I pictured Brian accepting this atrocious gift and tried to force a smile. "How nice," I said.

Kirk patted me on the shoulder just before getting in the car. "Don't worry," he said. "Everything will work out."

I thought of my family and the heartbreak we had ahead of us. I could only pray that Nick could somehow be stopped and turned around. No matter what he had done, I wanted so much for Nick to come back to the family who loved him.

CHAPTER 13

ANDY AND EDITH'S
EXCELLENT ADVENTURE

"What is that sickening smell?" Stony whispered to Kirk as we drove off. Kirk shook his head and rolled down his window. I knew what it was: Edith's car freshener earrings. Last month at our homemaking meeting, she showed the women how to make earrings from the little cardboard pine trees people hang from their radio knobs.

"Perfume and jewelry all in one!" she had announced, as if this were the idea of the century. Now here she was, giving us a pine-scented overdose as she sat in the backseat with huge green trees hanging from her ears.

"Well, whatever the smell is, it'll be gone in a wink thanks to my earrings," Edith beamed.

Stony turned around, saw the source of the stench, and forced a polite smile. Then he rolled down *his* window.

Edith winked and whispered to me, "I have some banana ones in my purse, too."

After buying us dinner at a smaller airport, Kirk and Stony stood guard at the door to the ladies' room while Edith and I went in.

"Boy, nobody better bad-mouth the airlines to me," Edith said, washing her hands. "I've never seen service like this in my life!"

I smiled. It must be interesting to be like Edith and not be earthbound.

"They even watch outside the door, to make sure we're okay," she went on.

And to make sure I don't use the telephone, I thought to myself.

"And now, a private jet—Wow!" Edith was having the time of her life. As we joined up with the agents again, Edith said, "Hey, perk up, Andy. What's the matter?"

"I . . . I guess I just miss my family," I said.

"We'll have a fuel stop in New York," Stony said, "Then we'll have you to England before you know it."

"You know there's a fuel conspiracy," Edith said. "You can make cheaper fuel out of cow manure, but the big oil companies are hoarding it so no one can find out."

Stony just stared at Edith. "The oil companies are hoarding cow manure?"

"What do you think," she said, "those giant refinery tanks have *oil* in them? Ha!" Edith lowered her voice as if sharing a big secret. "They pay farmers to gather up the cow pies and ship them all to Texas."

Stony was rolling his eyes and trying to change the subject.

"Hey—" Edith said, "Why do you think it stinks when you drive past a refinery?"

Maybe, I thought, because everyone inside is wearing scented earrings.

Stony clenched his jaw. "I can't talk to this woman," he muttered to Kirk and walked off.

Kirk sighed and led us to the runway.

It was dark by the time Edith and I climbed on board the roomy jet. The macaw was already bobbing and bowing in his cage which had been placed in a lounge area toward the back of the plane. Sure, give him the safest spot, I thought to myself.

"So what!" the bird cackled, as if it had read my mind. It had already treated Kirk and Stony to an assortment of its unprintable vocabulary on the way. Kirk had nearly run the car off the road, thinking Edith or I was cussing him out.

Now Angel began singing, "It's a Small World." Edith joined right in and neither one was on key.

"What say we cover old Mr. Angel?" Kirk said, offering Edith a blanket.

"Beddy-bye time," she cooed, covering the macaw with tender affection.

Another man climbed onto the plane. "This is Major Devin O'Malley, our pilot," Kirk said.

The pilot extended his hand. "Ladies." His blue eyes formed crescents when he smiled, and his Adam's apple moved when he spoke.

"Once we're in the air, I suggest you and Edith get some sleep," Kirk said. "After we land, you can call home for messages and see if your husband has left you any information."

I nodded. I couldn't imagine sleeping with all I had to worry about, but the exhaustion of the day finally won out, and I dozed off.

"I don't want you to worry," I heard someone whisper, startling me awake.

"Huh?" I was still half dreaming and sat up. Except for a few cabin lights, the plane was dark. "Who is it?" I said.

"Kirk. We need to make an emergency landing, but I don't want you to be alarmed."

"What? What's wrong?"

"Some minor engine trouble. We're over Pennsylvania now, and we'll have to set down on an isolated road."

"On a road?! Not at an airport?"

"It's okay. Our pilots are trained for emergencies like this. But you and Miss Horvitz better buckle up."

Edith was rubbing her eyes and fumbling for her seat belt.

"What on earth—" I said, staring out the window at the farms below. There were no lights anywhere—only gray shadows of trees and barns in pale moonlight.

The jet came down fast, bumping hard against the road. Trees and fences whipped by as we slowed down, the engine shrieking against the stillness of the night outside. Major O'Malley brought the plane to a stop outside a darkened farmhouse.

"Stay here while we check this out," Kirk said, as he and the other two hopped out of the plane. Out my window I could see fireflies bobbing. Then suddenly they grew brighter and I realized I was seeing the flames of gas lanterns that two men were carrying as they ran toward us.

"You got trouble?" I heard one man shout. Edith was rummaging around as I listened to muffled men's voices. I couldn't hear them distinctly, but it seemed the men were trying to help.

"You don't suppose we'll explode, do you?" Edith asked.

I was grateful when Stony poked his head back into the plane just then and asked us to come with him. I was out of there like a rocket. Edith was right on my heels, dragging her purse, the trash bag, and Angel with her.

Stony introduced us to the farmers, then said, "We're in luck. This is Amish country." No wonder all the farms had looked so dark, without any electricity. And, I noticed, no power lines were overhead to block the landing. Though the Amish farmers didn't know much about jet engines, they nevertheless had an extensive supply of tools and were most eager to help us get on our way.

"We should have this going by dawn," Major O'Malley said to Kirk. One of the farmers invited Edith and me into his home, where his wife greeted us warmly and led us to a spare bedroom.

"I'll get the light," Edith offered, feeling her way along the wall. "Hey, where is it?" Edith obviously didn't know about this way of life.

The Amish woman smiled, lit a gas lamp, and pulled it over to the doorway. "This is the light we use," she said.

"Hey—neat antique," Edith said.

I sighed and hugged the Amish woman. "We appreciate this so much," I said. I glanced at Angel's covered cage and prayed he'd keep his beak buttoned.

"We were just about to sit down to breakfast," the woman said. "Our food is plain, but you're welcome to join us."

"At midnight?" Edith bellowed.

I glanced at my wristwatch. "Edith, it's four in Pennsylvania," I said.

"Okay, at four in the morning?" Edith went on, her eyes wide with amazement.

The Amish woman chuckled. "We're usually out working by now, but all the men are curious about your sudden arrival in our valley."

Terrific; we had just become another UFO sighting.

"So are you hungry?" the woman asked.

"I'll just have a Pop Tart," Edith chirped.

I cringed and the Amish woman frowned. "What's that?"

"Oh, anything you have will be fine, I'm sure," I said, nudging Edith. "But perhaps we should get some more rest, first." The woman nodded, showed us a pitcher of water and the basin for washing, then left us alone.

"What's the deal?" Edith asked me. "Have we gone back in time?" I tried to explain that the Amish lived a simpler life, avoiding modern inventions.

"You gotta be kidding," Edith said. "No cars, no TV?" Then she thought for a minute. "Actually, that makes a lot of sense. Televisions emit electro magneto partisan waves that eat the wiring in your walls. That's the real reason termite inspectors wear gas masks."

I sighed. "Gas masks, Edith?"

"Sure. As for cars, why we're just part of the cow manure conspiracy when we own one and fill it up with gasoline."

"You okay in there?" Kirk's voice was outside the farmhouse.

Relieved to be interrupted, I opened an outside door.

"Oh, these people are so gracious," I said. "How's the repair going?"

"The major thinks we'll be leaving before long. Why don't you two get some sleep, and we'll wake you when it's ready."

I closed the door and turned back to Edith. She was rummaging through her handbag. "I guess I grabbed the wrong stuff," she said, "but I thought that baby was gonna blow."

I sighed and looked out the window toward the plane where Kirk joined the others as they poked around the engine.

"What are you missing?" I asked her, thinking surely the answer would be "everything," since she'd had no time to pack.

"I always crochet myself to sleep," Edith said.

How handy, I thought: If you get cold, you can just whip up another blanket.

"And I never go anywhere without my medication or my yarn and hooks," she went on. "I had them out on the plane—plus a bunch of patterns and stuff—and when that one feller said to get out of the plane, I just grabbed everything I could get my hands on and shoved it into my bag." She was dumping the big purse upside down on the bed, shaking out its contents. "But this ain't my stuff."

I looked at the envelopes and papers that were fluttering to the floor and started to pick them up. "Here," I said, "They must belong to the, uh, airline men. Let's take them back out and get your yarn and—"

Suddenly, my eyes fell on the name "Butler, Nick" printed on the top of one page. I held it under the light of the gas lamp to get a better look. There, below his name, was a list of CIA operations he had headed up, with dates in the left margin—some as recent as six months ago:

Intercepted Montoya shipment—Colombia/Miami, Grounded three Montoya aircraft—Managua/Corpus

Christi, Successful sting operation netting fifteen top Montoya agents, confiscating weapons arsenal and half-ton raw cocaine.... On and on it went, listing what appeared to me to be reasons for Francisco Montoya to want to kill Nick, not to hire him.

My hands were shaking. "Edith, let me see those," I said, scooping up the rest of the scattered papers, and holding them under the light.

"Why—what are they?" Edith asked.

"Oh, just ... " quick—*think*! "Just various travel itineraries," I said. "You know ... tour ideas. What to see in England and such."

Edith shrugged. "Any fool knows what you see in England," she said. "Buckingham Palace, London Bridge, and Uncle Ben."

(Well, one out of three's not bad).

Thankfully, Edith began to undress and get into bed. "I'm gonna forget about crocheting tonight," she said. "I'm too tired."

"Do you, uh, mind if I look over these papers?" I asked. "Will the light keep you awake?"

Edith chuckled. "That dim ol' thing? It's a wonder you can read at all." She turned over and mumbled, "If I was Amish, I'd sneak me in a generator and some decent lights." I could just see Edith Horvitz selling black market extension cords to the less-active Amish.

As Edith nodded off, I pored over the papers—there was a photo and description of Nick, newspaper clippings of the trouble he'd caused Montoya, and in one envelope, a stack of passports bearing Kirk's and Stony's pictures, but each with a different name. One scrap of paper listed Nick's trip to Africa, then England and a question mark. Finally there was a list of names, with Nick's crossed out in red ink and initialed "F. M."

Suddenly, I felt sick again and ran from the house, out into the night.

CHAPTER 14

SECRET AGENT ANDY

I found my way to the privacy of a thick hedge and, completely setting aside my fear of spiders, darted into it. Between bouts of nausea, I prayed for help. How could I have so easily trusted two complete strangers and believed their lies about my brother? And here I was, helping them find him! I felt so ashamed, so stupid. Why did I have to blurt out information about the fireside? Had I put the missionaries in danger as well?

"Please, God," I silently prayed, "help me think of a way to warn Nick that Montoya's henchmen are after him. And please, help me come out of this alive."

I've got to find a telephone, I thought. And then I remembered, the Amish have no phones! No wonder Kirk and Stony weren't worried about leaving Edith and me alone. I had no idea how far it was into town or if I could make it back in time to board the plane again.

Should I tell Edith? No, there was no predicting her reaction. I'd have to keep my knowledge a secret and pretend to go along with their plans. Kirk and Stony—or whoever they really were—would probably keep Edith and me alive until we could lead them to Nick. But then, since we'd be witnesses, they'd probably kill us, too. Or maybe not Edith, since her mental state would keep her from being much of a threat as a witness. What luck—saved by insanity, I thought.

And no one at home would even miss me, since they thought I was on vacation in Europe anyway. My family would call home from England, not reach me, and assume I was out doing Relief Society work. Not one soul knew where I was right now.

My stomach finally settled down, and I was just about to go back in the house when I noticed two men walking away from the plane, coming toward the hedge. I glanced back at the door to the bedroom and realized I couldn't make it there without them seeing me, so I froze.

As they got closer, I could hear Kirk's and Stony's voices. "Are you kidding," Kirk said, "she has no clue. We found her stuck in a doggie door, remember?"

I wished I could have heard their plans, but they walked around the back of the farmhouse. I took a deep breath and prayed for a plan. First, I had to get the papers back into the airplane, so Kirk and Stony wouldn't suspect that I was on to them. After waiting a while, I stepped out of the hedge and walked to the bedroom, stepped in, and carefully closed the door. My heart was pounding like a piston. Loading my purse with the documents, I turned to go back outside.

"What's happenin', baby?" a voice said.

A scream caught in my throat and I fell to the ground. Then Angel squawked and I began to breathe again. It was only that stupid bird. I glanced back at Edith, who was still snoring softly.

Stepping out into the moonlight again, I walked in the direction of the plane, acting unhurried and trying to keep my legs from shaking. Everything was silent. I resisted the urge to look behind me and just kept walking. Then, just as I was nearing the plane, a door flew open and a bright light went on. This time I screamed.

"Mrs. Taylor?" It was Major O'Malley.

"Oh," I said, swallowing hard, "you scared me."

"What are you doing up? I thought you and Miss Horvitz were sleeping."

"Well, I . . . I just couldn't rest," I said. "So I . . . I thought I may as well load my things and wait on the plane."

Major O'Malley stared at me with those penetrating blue eyes. Then he smiled and reached for my purse. "Let me give you a hand," he said.

I hesitated, terrified that he'd see the contents of my purse, then handed the purse up to him anyway. He tossed it onto a seat, then reached down to give me a hand up. "Thank-you," I said, and sat down quickly with my purse. "I . . . I hope I'm not interrupting you. Were you asleep?"

"No, no. Just going over some things. We're actually ready to leave."

I was struck with the sudden thought that perhaps they were planning to leave Edith and me snoozing in a remote Amish village while they took off for England without us. But then, we'd probably be able to find a town and a telephone before they could make it to England.

"All fixed, huh?" I said. It was only four-thirty.

"Yep." Major O'Malley turned back to a tool case he had in the cockpit, and I glanced around for Edith's yarn and patterns. Wherever she had unloaded them, had to be where the papers originally were. My eyes scanned the plane looking for Edith's things. I could just imagine Kirk and Stony looking for their missing papers and finding a pile of yarn in their place.

Just then the major came out of the cockpit and grabbed a dark leather jacked he'd thrown on the floor. Putting it on, he hopped out of the plane and began checking something outside. I almost gasped—the pile of yarn had been under his coat.

Quickly, I loaded Edith's yarn, patterns, and other paraphernalia into my purse, then placed the papers in the spot where I assumed they'd been before. Climbing out of the plane, I said, "If we're ready to leave, I can go get Edith. I . . . I found some yarn she was missing, also."

"Yeah, okay." Major O'Malley was busy on the other side of the plane.

Walking fast, I headed for the bedroom. As I opened the door, I heard a phone ringing! Maybe I *could* warn Nick! Then I realized it was Angel and my heart sank.

"Edith," I whispered, "it's time to go. And I found your yarn."

She sat up. "Oh, good. My stuff! Where was it?"

"On the plane. I was just out there and they're ready to take off again."

"Is this a wild trip or what?" Edith asked, slipping into her yellow housecoat again.

I smiled. She didn't know the half of it.

"So did you wake up happy wappy?" she asked.

"Which timey wimey?" I asked.

Edith laughed. I wanted so much to tell her the whole story, but how could I commiserate with someone who refuses to miserate?

Angel was still mimicking a telephone when Kirk began banging on our door. "Are you ladies awake?"

I opened the door and Kirk stepped right in, glancing nervously around. I stared at him with new eyes, knowing his real intentions now. I turned away so he wouldn't see the fear and disgust in my eyes. "I thought I heard a phone ringing," Kirk said.

"Oh, that's Angel," Edith said. "Ain't he good?"

Kirk sighed, visibly relieved. "Come on. Let's load up."

The generous Amish people had prepared a basket of food for us to take along and stood waving in their dark clothes as we taxied down their road. Lifting into the sky, I prayed again for some way to warn Nick. "Will we still be stopping in New York?" I asked Kirk.

"Yes. We still have to refuel."

"Oh, shopping—great," Edith exclaimed. "I've always wanted to go shopping in New York."

Kirk smiled. "Stopping, not shopping."

Edith frowned. "Oh."

"Maybe I could check for messages," I said, still trying not to look directly at Kirk or Stony.

"Yes. Maybe your husband has called," Stony said.

I sat back in my seat and stared out the window. Brian . . . the love of my life. Would I ever see him or the children again? I pictured them innocently checking into Nick's surprise hotel, the kids bouncing on the beds, Brian and Nick joking about my getting left behind. And darling Nick, my baby brother whose heroism might just cost him his life. What would my children do if I didn't make it through this?

I imagined my funeral, the hurt and confusion on my children's faces, the anguish in Brian's heart as he'd try to go on and raise the kids without me. I thought of the beautiful teachings of the gospel, and the comfort it is to know that we'd all be together again someday. But it's still difficult to be separated by death; you still long for the relationship, for the touch of a hand, for a listening ear.

How deeply I loved them all! How desperately I wanted to see them again.

"Mrs. Taylor," Kirk said, putting his hand on my shoulder. "Are you all right?"

He had startled me, and I jumped. "Oh—yes." Suddenly conscious that I was crying, I wiped my tears with the back of my hand. I had to think quickly. "I'm just so disappointed in Nick," I whispered.

Kirk squeezed my arm. "I know. It was a shock to all of us." That filthy, lying crook, I thought. It sickened me to have him touch my sleeve. "But you're doing the right thing," Kirk said, "helping us find him in time."

Right—before he ices the queen of England. What a stupid story—talk about a tank of cow manure. That was probably why they stepped into the hall when I told them Nick was already in England—they needed to make up a reason for chasing after him.

Montoya probably had the patience of a Mafia kingpin and wanted Nick eliminated immediately, not to hear some feeble excuse about waiting for him to get back from Europe. No wonder Kirk could arrange for a private jet at the snap of a finger; Montoya's money was probably matched only by his determination to rid himself of his enemies. And they agreed so fast to bring

Edith along when she wouldn't hand over her camera no doubt because Montoya would not be amused to see photos of Nick's killers on the front page of the newspaper.

It also explained how Major O'Malley brought the plane down so easily on a rural road; he probably made most of his landings in cocaine fields.

I prayed again, and this time I felt a surge of strength. Part of me was welling up in anger at these criminals, and part of me was flat-out determined to stop them and rescue my brother. The tears of pity were dry, now. I suddenly felt myself brimming with determination, charged with a resolve to beat these gangsters at their own game. And I only prayed that I'd know how I was going to do it.

CHAPTER 15

MISSIONARY IMPOSSIBLE

When we touched down in New York, Kirk and Stony walked us into the terminal to find a phone. With the pilots' strike still on, it was eerily empty. But a gift shop was open, and Edith bolted right in.

"I love New York," she bellowed, reading the message on cups and T-shirts. "I love New York, I love New York."

I smiled. Edith didn't even know New York. But she was loading up on oversized sleep shirts, apple earrings, and a cardboard Statue of Liberty crown.

Kirk and Stony looked at me as if I could control her somehow. "Hey," I shrugged, "you wanted to bring her."

Kirk followed Edith into the store. "We really don't have time to shop," he said.

"Oh, keep your socks on. I'm almost done," Edith said, waving a New York Yankees banner. Then she dumped her souvenirs on the counter and said, "Oops—I left my purse on the plane!"

By then, Kirk was completely unnerved and eager to get on our way with no static from Edith. "Here!" he barked, peeling some twenties out of his wallet. "You need some other clothes anyway, I guess."

Edith's eyes absolutely danced. "Well, I'll be!" she hooted. "For the life of me, I can't figure why you airline folks get bad publicity." Edith then grabbed a snow globe, a chocolate Empire State Building (with King Kong attached), and a Mets baseball hat with a solar-powered fan built in. "Long as you're buying!" she

crowed. Then she slapped an entire display of sunflower seeds and pistachio nuts on the counter as well
"for Angel."

The clerk was stuffing Edith's purchases into a bag
as Edith kept rambling. "Why, I've never seen two
nicer, sweeter young fellas in my life. Isn't that right,
Andy?"

I gritted my teeth. "Right."

Stony led us to a telephone, and I dialed my answering machine. Eight messages. The first was a less-active
sister asking whether the church could buy her a house.
The second was someone asking to borrow the Relief
Society dish towels to shine cars with at a youth car
wash. The next was a visiting teacher letting me know
that Sister Granzigger's ovaries turned out to be just
fine. Kirk was listening in, and I watched his eyes grow
round with amazement.

The fourth call was Sister Dillon, explaining that
she'd just collected a bumper crop of garlic that she was
planning to bring on Sunday to distribute. The fifth call
was a member of the bishopric asking me to speak on
tribulation (a subject I was researching this very
minute). The next call was Elroy Morganstern letting
me know that his sister and her kids were coming into
town, and could they stay at my house.

After Elroy was Claudia Lambert with a pig report.
"He's getting so fat, he can't even fit through the doggie
door anymore," she said. (First I have my I. Q. in common with Gizmo the dog, and now I have my figure in
common with Curly the pig.)

The eighth call was Brian. It scared me to have Kirk
listening; I didn't want him to find out where they were
staying.

"Hi, sweetie." Brian's voice sounded wonderful. "We
made it to England. Sure miss you. I understand the
pilots are still on strike, so I'll call again when we hear
word that it's ended and see if you can get a flight out.
This is crazy, huh, babe? Well, the kids all miss you,

and—" then I could hear the kids shouting, "Hi, Mom! I love you! Me too, Mom!" I tried to breathe with a lump in my throat. Then Brian came back on again. "I love you, Andy. Talk to you soon I hope—Bye!"

Kirk muttered something under his breath, then saw me watching him and said, "Well, looks like we still don't know where they are." I tried not to show my immense relief and shrugged. "We'll call again from London," Kirk said.

On the flight to England, Edith crocheted an orange bow tie for Stony and a pink one for Kirk. "Whatcha think?" she asked, holding them up. "I think they deserve these, don't you?"

I couldn't help smiling as I pictured those villains finally getting something they deserved. "They're perfect," I said.

"Here's a little thank-you," Edith announced, walking to the front where Kirk and Stony were sitting. As she knotted the ties around their necks I couldn't help wishing she'd give each one a hard yank and choke them.

Kirk and Stony exchanged snickers and pulled the ties off as soon as Edith began dozing.

I tiptoed to the front. "You know," I whispered, "I've been thinking about that fireside tonight and how you guys can blend in, and I think your best chance is to look like missionaries. And," I said, picking up the garish ties, "all missionaries wear ties."

Kirk and Stony stared at each other for a minute, thinking. Kirk was chewing his cheek. "I don't know," he said. And then, "I guess we should look like we fit in." Reluctantly, he took the ties. "All right."

I studied them for a minute. "Do you guys have white shirts?"

"White shirts?"

"Oh, absolutely," I said. "Missionaries have a distinct look, and a white shirt is essential," I said.

"We can pick some up when we land," Stony said.

"If there's time," Kirk added. "Wait." He opened a duffel bag and pulled out a white Polo shirt.

"That will do with a jacket," I said. "But Stony still needs one. And they wear their hair cut much shorter than yours."

"We have to get haircuts?" Stony was aghast.

I gave them a helpless look and shrugged. "No moustaches, either."

"What?!"

"Sorry—mission regulations."

Kirk smacked Stony in the arm. "Hey—you'd blow this for a moustache? Come on."

Stony sighed. "What else?"

I pretended to be studying them when the macaw squawked, "Serves you right!" I bit my lip to keep from laughing. Then Angel began mimicking a garbage disposal again, and woke Edith up. "Who's there—who's there?" she said, startled out of a dream.

"Just us," I said. "You had a good nap. Edith, these nice airline officials want to go with us to a church fireside. Isn't that great?"

"Depends who's speaking," Edith said.

I sighed. Good old Edith always says what she thinks. "My brother, Nick, will be speaking," I said.

"Oh—he's the one who spoke at homemaking meeting the night I showed the women how to kill snails with beer."

Kirk and Stony squinted, speechless.

"Oh, you'll love Nick," Edith said, coming up front to join us. "He is so smart and has such a great personality."

I watched as Kirk and Stony forced smiles.

"Are you thinking of becoming Mormons?" Edith asked.

Kirk and Stony squirmed. "Uh . . . yes," Kirk lied. "That's why we'd like to attend tonight."

"Well, first thing you gotta do," Edith said, pulling a pack of cigarettes from Stony's pocket and crunching them between her palms, "is get rid of these babies."

Stony gasped, but Kirk put a calming hand on Stony's arm.

"It's a fireside for missionaries," I told Edith, "and I thought they'd feel most comfortable if they blended in with the crowd and looked like elders."

"Everybody's going to look like Elvis?" Edith hooted.

I could just picture a whole chapel filled with black-haired Elder Presleys wearing rhinestone jackets and bell-bottom pants.

"No, *elders*," I said.

"What is it—a room full of old people?" Stony asked.

"No—that's what we call our missionaries," I said. "In fact, if you really want to fit in, you should wear name tags."

Stony shook his head. "This is too much."

"Oh, stop whining," Edith said. "Nobody likes a crybaby. Here, I'll make you some name tags. Where are your coats?"

Kirk and Stony dug through their luggage for jackets and handed them over to Edith. She printed "Elder Emery" and "Elder Melendez" on two slips of paper, then glued them onto the lapels with some of the special glue she was bringing to Brian.

"Presto!" Edith said, admiring her handiwork. "You'll be the best lookin' elders in the whole room!" Then she winked at me and whispered, "And those tags'll stay on for life!"

16

THE GOLDEN OPPORTUNITY

"I feel just like Mary Poppins," Edith announced cheerily as we circled the airport in heavy fog. She had changed into her knee-length "I Love New York" night shirt and was wearing the apple earrings and the Statue of Liberty crown.

Kirk's nostrils flared as he set his jaw and waited for clearance to land. "What time do you think the fireside is?" he asked me for the fourth time.

"I just won't know until I can call the mission home," I said. "But I think it will probably be around seven-thirty or so."

"We won't have time to check your messages," Kirk said. "We'll just have to go directly to the fireside."

Stony kept popping in and out of the cockpit, always emerging with a long face and shaking his head. "Not yet," he'd say.

Edith began singing, "Just a spoonful of sugar helps the medicine go down," and just as I thought Kirk was about ready to leap from his seat and strangle her, we heard Major O'Malley shout, "We're going in!"

Hell's Angel began another unprintable tirade, and I wished Edith would keep singing to drown him out. Finally we touched the runway. As Major O'Malley brought us speeding in, Edith said, "Wow—my cheeks feel like they're gettin' a face lift!"

Even before we came to a stop, Kirk was tossing luggage and motioning us to come along quickly. Major

O'Malley barely stuck his head out of the cockpit to say good-bye, as we hurried down the exit steps. While Stony arranged for a car and picked up a white shirt, Kirk led Edith and me to a telephone.

Everything was a blur as we dashed into the airport. My heart sank as we hurried past some uniformed English bobbies, and I knew I couldn't ask for their help.

"It's at seven," I said to Kirk, hanging up with the mission office. "What's London time right now?"

"Six!" he growled, stuffing the address into his pocket and urging us to jog along beside him. "Are you sure we have to cut our hair?"

I tried to look desperate. "I really don't think you'll get in, otherwise," I lied. "Women can dress how they want, but the codes for men are very strict." Thank heavens Edith, who had only recently been activated, knew nothing about mission regulations and figured I was telling the truth.

Kirk stopped and looked both ways in the terminal. There was no barber shop anywhere in sight. "We'll never make it."

"Hey," Edith said, "I went to barber school; I can cut your hair."

Kirk clearly had his doubts and glanced back at me. I shrugged and said, "It's worth a try."

Soon he and Stony were sitting on the fender of the car as Edith used her dull craft scissors to snip at their hair. "I hope this doesn't wreck my scissors," she said, cutting away uneven hunks. Her scissors couldn't have been in worse shape if they'd been used to cut the particle board for her house.

I turned away, unable to keep from snickering as I watched those goons get sheared by a woman who could scatter an entire flock of sheep just by pulling scissors from her purse. She even managed to whack off most of Stony's mustache. I kept hoping Edith would nip off one of their ears and cause us to go to a hospital instead of to the fireside, but finally she announced the job was finished, and they brushed themselves off.

"Now," Edith said, studying her work. "You look just like Mormon missionaries."

Kirk and Stony stared in disbelief at each other's hideous haircuts, decided to make the best of it, and climbed into the car. Kirk gripped the steering wheel with white knuckles, trying to remember to drive on the left side of the street.

"You sure you went to barber school?" Stony asked, feeling the prickly stubble behind his ears.

"Hey," Edith said. "I went for awhile. I never said I graduated."

Stony shook his head, glancing over at Kirk and muttering. He flipped down the visor mirror, saw his hair and his reduced mustache and jumped. "You call this a haircut?" he shrieked. "I look like Hitler!"

Just then Edith began shaking sunflower seeds into Angel's cage and spilling half of them into the backseat.

"Hey—*now* what are you doing?" Stony yelled.

Edith looked up, completely unfazed by Stony's anger. "I'm feeding the bird," she said. "They have to eat, you know."

Stony turned to Kirk and began screaming, "You call this a haircut? You call this a haircut?" until Kirk pulled over on the left and motioned for Stony to get out of the car with him. The two of them stood behind the car arguing, and I glanced in front to see if they'd left the keys in the ignition. I wasn't sure I had the guts to drive off and leave them there, but the thought occurred to me. As it turned out, it wasn't an option anyway. I looked out the back window and saw Kirk holding the keys as he shook his hand at Stony.

"That one sure is a crybaby," Edith said.

"Crybaby," echoed the macaw.

Oh, great, I thought. Another priceless phrase to add to Angel's collection.

Kirk and Stony got back into the car, Stony visibly trying to control himself and breathing deeply. "Right after the operation," he whispered to Kirk.

"What operation?" Edith asked. "Did you have an operation?"

"Yes, he did," Kirk answered, thinking quickly. "He had appendicitis."

"Oh, boy," Edith said. "You better watch out. A friend of mine had suspender-itis, and a month later—whammo!—she dropped dead of a massive confection. Her skin broke out in all these gooey, yellow sores an' boy, when those puppies popped, did they smell . . . "

Stony was clenching his teeth trying to tolerate Edith's stupid, grisly story. I stared out the window and prayed again for help.

Kirk pulled over again and asked me to get out of the car for a moment. "First," he said, "We really appreciate your help. I know it was a big adjustment for you to learn the truth about Nick, and I think you're holding up great."

"Well, if I can help you capture him without anyone getting hurt, then I'll do what I can," I said.

"That's what I was coming to," he said. "Is there any way you can get Miss Horvitz to . . . you know . . . be quiet or something?"

I bit my lip, pretending to think. "I just don't know," I said.

"Can you keep her distracted once we get to the fireside?"

Kirk asked. "Keep her in the parking lot, maybe?"

I gulped. That definitely did not fit into my plan. "Well, wouldn't you rather have me inside helping you fit in?"

"What more can you do?" Kirk asked. "We look the part, right?"

I stared at his crocheted tie and swallowed. "Oh, yes, but what if someone asks you a question, or . . . or they have some ritual and you don't know what to do?"

Kirk thought for a moment. "Actually, it might help for Nick to see you with me. I mean, it's been a few years and he might not recognize me—with the haircut and all."

I nodded sympathetically. "I'll keep Edith beside me during the meeting," I suggested.

"Please," Kirk said, and started back to the car.

"Um," I said, "Exactly how are you planning to make Nick think you're on his side?" I swallowed again and prayed Kirk would give me some information.

"Oh, leave that up to us," he said.

"I guess you'd want to talk to him after the meeting, huh?"

I hoped they were planning to be a little more discreet than to walk right in and shoot him.

"We'll see." Kirk smiled.

I got back into the car and tried to keep my hands from shaking. Stony's words, "right after the operation," were ringing through my ears—did he mean he'd kill us as soon as they had taken care of Nick? Between Edith and that macaw, I was surprised they hadn't done away with her yet. She had clearly pushed Stony to the brink.

"I suppose you fellas know the importance of fiber in your diet," Edith said.

Stony shook his head in disbelief and kept staring out his window. Kirk ignored her, watching for road signs and reading the written directions we'd gotten on the phone.

"That's why Angel will live to be a hundred," Edith went on. "It's all that birdseed. I take it myself, you know."

I sighed. Who but Edith would eat actual birdseed?

"Oh, yeah, I sprinkle it on just about everything," she said. "I'm thinking of writing a cookbook, too. It scrapes all the gunk off your intestines," she said. "They get all gummed up, you know."

Kirk grimaced and Stony began grinding his teeth.

"If you scrape a little bird dropping off your windshield—you know, while it's still sticky, and rub it between your fingers, you'll see that bird doo is nice and loose—"

"Edith—" I said, feeling queasier by the minute, "could this story wait a little bit? It's kind of—"

"See? There you go," Edith chuckled. "Everybody wants to procrastinate having the right diet. People think that if they can't see their intestines, they don't exist."

"Miss Horvitz—" Kirk said, his patience thinning quickly.

"Okay, okay," Edith bellowed. "But you show me one constipated bird."

We all just sat there, speechless.

"See?" Edith said, sticking her chin triumphantly in the air, "You can't do it."

With a great sigh, Kirk stared at the road ahead and tried to tune her out.

Edith then launched into a rousing rendition of "I Am Woman Hear Me Roar." I don't know if I will ever again see photos of the streets of London without mentally hearing Edith's crackly version of this song.

Kirk turned the last corner and pulled over. "Finally," he said, and turned off the engine. "Here we are."

I felt my stomach flip over as I looked at the brick building. It was seven-fifteen. I closed my eyes and thought another prayer.

"Guess I'll leave Angel in the foyer," Edith said, climbing out with him, her purse, and the trash bag.

Shaking and clammy, I climbed the steps to the meetinghouse, leading Kirk and Stony. Faint strains of men's voices singing "Called to Serve" echoed out onto the street. As we came through the doors at the back of the chapel, my eyes searched frantically for Nick.

"Do you see him?" Kirk whispered.

I shook my head. Nick wasn't seated on the stand. "Let's sit down," I whispered, "and I'll keep looking."

Kirk and Stony glanced around as they slid onto a bench in the back, with Edith and me between them.

As the song ended, an older gentleman (the mission president?) went to the podium and announced that

before introducing the special speaker, he'd like to set a
spiritual tone by beginning the meeting with voluntary
testimonies. Suddenly I was standing up. "That means
visitors," I said, climbing past Kirk's legs. "We have to
get right up there."

"What?!" Kirk whispered, reaching for my arm as I
took off down the aisle.

The mission president stared as I dashed up onto the
stand. Believe me, I thought to myself as I stared back
into the president's face, you cannot possibly be more
surprised than I am. *What am I doing?* I screamed
silently inside my head.

Kirk and Stony were right behind me, their heads
jerking around in complete confusion, as they followed
me and pulled Edith along with them.

"Just sit down," I whispered to Kirk as he bounded
up the stairs behind me, "and do what I do."

Trying to look unruffled, Kirk and Stony sat confi-
dently down on the stand. Edith adjusted her crown and
sat down with the huge red "I Love New York" heart
stretching over her ample bust line. Still startled, the
mission president sank slowly into his own seat, and
watched with his mouth hanging open as I stepped to
the microphone.

"Elders," I said, "my name is Andy Taylor and I'm a
Relief Society president from California." I was hoping
to ease the mission president's mind that I was not just
some mental patient who stumbled in off the street.

A small gasp went up from the front row, and I
glanced down. There were Brian, the kids, Nick, and
Zan! Every one of them was staring at me in absolute
disbelief, stunned smiles frozen on their upturned
faces.

"I am so grateful for this opportunity to bear my testimony and to thank you wonderful missionaries for the
great job you're doing," I said. I then mentioned how
thrilled I was to see my family and be reunited with
them, then I bore a brief testimony and concluded with,

"I've brought some visitors tonight, who would like to bear their testimonies about Joseph and Hyrum Smith."

Then, still having no clue as to what I was saying or doing, I stepped back to Kirk and Stony and whispered, "Just go to the mike and talk about Joseph Smith and Hyrum Smith as if you know them really well. No one will suspect a thing."

"But who are they?" Kirk whispered, "the cough drop brothers?"

"Church leaders," I said.

"Do we go up together?" Stony asked.

I nodded and motioned them to the podium.

Kirk swallowed, his eyes clearly round with panic.

Flustered, he stood up and cleared his throat. Bringing Edith with him, he nodded at Stony to come, also.

Edith grabbed the mike and pulled it to her maroon-lipsticked mouth. "And I'd just like all you fellas to know that these two men bought me the clothes I'm wearing," she said, brimming with pride. "They are one hundred percent responsible for how I look."

An audible gasp arose from the entire congregation as they beheld the unforgettable Edith in all her glory. Okay, so maybe the mission president was not so certain, after all, that we weren't mental patients who stumbled in off the street.

I stepped up to Edith and smilingly pulled her back down to sit beside me, leaving Kirk and Stony together at the microphone.

With Kirk's and Stony's backs to us, I was able to pull a pen, and a note I had written earlier, from my pocket. Folding the paper over, I wrote on the outside, "Nick Butler—Urgent" and handed it to the mission president.

Kirk straightened his neon-colored bow tie and cleared his throat. "I was in Utah chatting with Joseph Smith the other day," he said, "after a game of tennis."

The missionaries burst into laughter and Kirk's knees began shaking. "He's not only a great leader, but has a great backhand," Kirk continued. Another roar of laughter.

I noticed the mission president stepping quietly aside
and motioning to Nick, who ducked down and hurried
quickly up the steps of the stand. Either they didn't recognize him from his photo, or they were too nervous to
notice, but neither Kirk nor Stony saw Nick slip in
behind them, sit down, and unfold my note.

"Run! Montoya hired these men to kill you," it said.

"And Mr. Smith sends his best regards," Kirk continued. He whipped around to glare at me, but I just
smiled and gave him the O.K. sign.

"They love you!" I whispered, grinning enthusiasti-
cally.

Now Stony was shoving his hands nervously into his
pockets and leaning in to the microphone. "I met Hymie
Smith on a flight to, uh, Dallas," Stony said. Now the
elders were whooping, thinking the whole thing was a
comedy act. "We had a nice, long chat over a cup of cof-
fee," he went on.

I glanced over at Nick, who was folding the note
back up and tucking it into his jacket. What was he
doing, still sitting there?! I caught his eye, gave him a
terrified look, and nodded my head toward the exit—
Get out, I wanted to scream—Run for your life!

Nick smiled and waved back at me. How could he
react so calmly? I stared at the floor and prayed that
Nick would come to his senses and dash out of the room.

The missionaries were laughing again, this time
because Stony made some comment about "Hymie"
Smith driving him to his hotel and what a heck of a
guy he was. He had even "paid off on the football bet"
they made on the plane.

Suddenly Nick was walking towards his killers! I
gasped and shook my head. "Run!" I mimed silently, but
he ignored me.

Stepping up behind Kirk and Stony, Nick put an arm
around each man's shoulders, and leaned in to the
microphone. Kirk and Stony froze in place, unsure just
what Nick would do next and perhaps unsure whether
this man was even Nick at all.

"Elders, you can tell these are special men, can't you?"

Kirk glanced back at me, and I somehow held a smile, as if their talks had gone perfectly.

Nick continued. "They're special because they're here looking into our religion, and they're thinking of becoming members." Then he looked side to side at Kirk and Stony. "Isn't that right?" Nick asked.

Kirk and Stony nodded at each other. "Definitely," Kirk said, looking utterly serious.

"So let's not keep them waiting," Nick said. "I'd like to invite every one of you elders to come up on the stand right now and give them the best Mormon greeting you can."

Stony glanced back at me and I shrugged, as if this was the normal procedure any visitor should expect.

The missionaries were smiling and looking timidly at each other, unsure whether to walk up onto the stand or not.

"Well, come on," Nick said. "On your feet! This is a golden opportunity, Elders! Which of you will be the one who gets a baptismal commitment?"

Suddenly, Kirk and Stony were surrounded by a sea of elders in white shirts, shoving and pushing, slapping them on their backs, shaking their hands, and talking to them all at once. One missionary was holding his flip-chart above the crowd, racing through the first discussion and turning pages faster than a card dealer shuffling a deck. It was complete bedlam.

Nick had somehow vanished, and Kirk and Stony were whipping their heads around, trying to find him, and struggling to break through the crowd. But the elders were yanking on their arms, shoving them back into the swarm, and shouting into their faces as fervently as they could, each one trying to drown out the next guy. They didn't even notice Edith's "Elder" stickers on Kirk's and Stony's lapels—or if they did see them, they figured the tags were all in fun, I suppose.

I wanted to grab Brian and the kids, and pull them away to safety, but just as I was making my way down to them, Nick grabbed my wrist and whispered, "I have their guns—you're safe. Call the police!" So I ran the other way, leaving Nick with the criminals and dashing to a pay phone in the hall.

After dialing, I glanced back at Kirk and Stony. I was barely able to see them through the crush of elders. But Edith was leaping from the stand—over the wooden railing—still lugging her trash bag. She caught up to me in a hallway, just as I was hanging up with the police.

"Hey, who does Nick think he is?" Edith barked, "taking all the credit for those investigators? *We're* the ones who brought 'em!"

I grabbed her by the arm and leaned into her face. "Those men aren't from the airline," I said in a low voice. "They're hired killers and they're after Nick."

"What?" Edith leaped into action. "My bird's in there!" And then, pulling away from my grasp, she bolted back toward the chapel.

"Edith—stop!" I screamed. But it was too late. The statue of liberty was bounding right back into the arms of danger.

17

ETERNAL BONDING

I ran back into the chapel after Edith, but she had disappeared into the crowd. Suddenly I saw Brian and the kids, and I fell into their arms, crying.

"Mom!" Ryan shrieked, throwing his arms around me and bursting into tears. "I missed you, Mom!"

Grayson and Erica dashed over to hug me, too, and I wept as I held them in a giant hug. "You're safe, you're safe," I found myself whispering, praying my thanks and stroking their hair as tears streamed down my cheeks.

"What's going on? How did you get here?" Brian asked.

"Where's Nick?" Zan asked. I looked at the hub of commotion, just as Nick was pushing back into the fray. Edith was yanking a huge missionary out of her way by the collar. Then she whipped a green squirt bottle from her trash bag and dove into the tumult.

"Edith!" I shrieked. "Get away!" Suddenly she grabbed Kirk's right hand, and squirted glue onto it. Then, before he even realized what was happening, she slapped his two hands together, cementing them into one big knot.

"Hey—" Kirk yelled. But Edith was already doing the same to Stony, and before either of them knew it, their hands appeared clasped in a permanent prayer. Suddenly, Kirk and Stony lunged out of the crowd and fell forward onto their knees, toppling over and scattering the elders. Nick had pushed them from behind, and while the baffled missionaries were caught with half a discussion still on their lips, Nick pointed one of the confiscated guns at the hoodlums and ordered them to stay put.

Both Kirk and Stony were sprawled on the floor with their hands stretched above their heads, as if handcuffed. As the mission president led the elders to the sides of the chapel, Edith emerged from the huddle, straightening her crown and wiping sweat from her forehead. She held the squirt bottle like a torch, high in the air.

"Hey—Sister Horvitz looks just like the Statue of Liberty," Grayson whispered.

"What is going on?" Brian asked.

"Why are Nick and Edith attacking those poor men?" Zan asked.

"Those men were trying to kill Nick," I panted.

"What?!" Brian gasped.

Zan dashed right to Nick's side. "Quick—give me a gun," she demanded.

Nick stared at her, almost in disbelief.

Zan leaned into his face, the corporate tiger ready to pounce. "I can do this," she said.

Nick pushed her—gently, but he definitely pushed her—to one side. "It's okay," he said, then smiling, "sweetheart."

Zan glared at his would-be attackers, looking ready to claw their eyes out, gun or no gun.

"Ha!" Edith was snarling right in Kirk's and Stony's faces. "That'll teach you to mess with Edith Horvitz!" Then she spun around, waved her squirt bottle, and announced to the crowd that she had glued the gangsters' hands together.

Sure enough, despite their obvious struggling, neither man seemed able to pull his hands apart. Edith then went behind them and squirted a stream of glue down the inside seams of their pants, and shoved their legs together. "They won't get far now," Edith said.

Nick beamed as he looked up at Edith and shook his head. "Good work," he said, stunned by Edith's daring.

Zan began lecturing the crooks, telling them in no uncertain terms what she would do to them if they ever came near her husband again, until finally Nick got her eye and waved her away.

"What is it with Mormon women?" Stony muttered to Kirk, "I'd rather face Montoya!"

Zan lifted her chin proudly and sniffed.

"What is going *on?*" Brian sputtered. I started to explain, but suddenly we heard English sirens and the screech of brakes as police cars converged outside. Then a dozen bobbies burst into the chapel, dashed over to Kirk and Stony, and pulled them to their feet. Unable to walk with their pant legs glued together, they had to hop like gunnysack racers.

Nick had taken pistols from their pockets when they were first jostled by the elders, and now he handed the guns over to the police as the crowd gasped. Grayson and Ryan were mesmerized.

"I couldn't let them put the elders in danger," I heard Nick say to the mission president as he explained how he'd managed to get the guns.

Zan proudly held his arm, then teasingly said, "You sure know how to keep the excitement in a marriage, Darling." They kissed, then Zan became serious and asked if this sort of thing could happen again.

"I hope not," Nick said, "but I've put a lot of bad people away. We'll just have to pray for God's protection, and have faith, Zan." He held her in a tender embrace.

As policemen were buzzing about concealed weapons, kidnapping charges, and previous warrants for arrest, Edith slung her bag of glue over one shoulder and paraded triumphantly before the captives. Kirk and Stony just glared, furious to have been beaten by someone like Edith Horvitz.

"You murderers think you can just run around killing people and leaving the bodies wherever you please," Edith said. "Do you have any idea what that costs taxpayers? Do you know how much the government would've had to pay to have our bodies picked up—let alone flown to California?" She whistled at the high price.

"And what do you think happens to the blood and guts—you think that just evaporates? Ha! Some poor street sweeper has to come and clean it all up."

Kirk and Stony just stared at her. But Edith wasn't through. "You ever priced a funeral?" she went on. Then she began to itemize the casket, the embalming, the makeup, the cemetery plot. (Obviously Edith should visit prisons and give lectures on the overlooked errors of one's ways, in particular, fiscal responsibility.)

As best I could, I summarized the last two days' events for Brian and the kids, who blinked with disbelief as I told them the details. Brian's eyes welled up with tears and he clutched me to his chest. "Andy," he whispered, "you could have been killed."

"Well, I tried not to think about that," I said. "Mostly I just prayed for a way to warn Nick."

Brian held me tight and whispered that he wouldn't know how to go on without me. "Come here," he said and motioned the kids to follow along. He took us into a vacant classroom and led us in a prayer of thanks. Then he held my hands to his lips as tears of gratitude rolled down his cheeks. "I love you, Andy. You always say Nick is the smart one, but I think he must have learned everything from you."

As we walked back to the chapel, we were met by a crush of newspaper reporters, blinding us with flashbulbs as they photographed Kirk and Stony being apprehended. One policeman was shaking hands with Edith, and after she whispered something in his ear, he yanked the pink and orange bow ties off the crooks and returned them to her.

The mission president was hugging Nick, his eyes brimming with tears of joy. "Elders," Nick then shouted into the crowd, "You just helped to apprehend two hit men for Francisco Montoya, one of the biggest drug lords in history."

The elders raised a giant cheer. "You're heroes!" Nick shouted. A reporter was scribbling down his every word.

"Brother Butler was going to speak to you about courage," the mission president said, his arm still around Nick's shoulders. "And I'd say we *saw* an excellent sermon tonight." Again, the elders clapped and cheered.

Then Nick turned to us. "Andy," he said, pointing across the room at me, "was the one who warned me about these men. She's a brave lady and I owe her my life." The elders cheered again.

My eyes filled with tears as I went over to Nick and threw my arms around his neck. Then I whispered in his ear, "I wonder if every little brother puts his big sister through times like this."

Nick laughed, then turned to Edith and said, "Sister Horvitz, you were a hero, too."

She smiled. "And I'm not done, yet. I brought a little gift for Brian, here!" Then suddenly, she whipped a fluffy auburn toupee (Brian is blond) out of her trash bag, squirted glue onto it, and slapped it onto the top of Brian's head faster than you can say "bad rug."

The elders whooped and cheered again.

"EDITH!" Brian screamed, "WHAT ARE YOU DOING?" He began tugging at the toupee, which wouldn't budge a hair.

"That's a better color on him, don't you think?" Edith asked the crowd of elders, as if they were a traveling team of color consultants.

Nick grinned and leaned in to Brian's gasping face. "That is one really bad piece," he smiled. "And I'm afraid you're going to have to wear it to the police station. They need us to go in with them."

A press photographer snapped a picture, and Brian looked ready to kill Edith. I smiled. "It looks fine, honey," I lied, my eyes watering as I tried not to bust up laughing. Erica, Grayson, and Ryan were all looking at their father with wrinkled noses.

Just then I felt dizzy again, no doubt proof that only one member of my family can handle the stress of spy work, and toppled against Brian as I slumped into a faint.

As I came to, I stared up into Brian's face and smiled.

"You look like Don King with a henna rinse," I mumbled.

Brian's eyes narrowed. "I just saved you from cracking your head open and this is the thanks I get?"

He helped me to my feet and I kissed him. "Now you know that no matter what happens to your looks," I said, "I'll always love you."

Brian smirked, then led me along as we followed the crowd into the foyer. "You sure you feel okay?" he asked.

"I'm fine," I assured him. "It's probably just the stress of this whole thing."

As the police dragged Kirk and Stony through the foyer to waiting cars, Angel blurted, "You call this a haircut?"

Brian whipped around, trying to pat the toupee flatter. Then he saw who had spoken the words, and did a double take. "It can't be ... it can't be ... " Brian stammered.

"Yep," Edith bellowed, picking up the cage. "That's my macaw. We brought him all the way from Los Angel-eeze."

Brian looked back at me and I offered a weak smile. "It's been an interesting trip," I said.

Once in the car, Brian began frowning and sniffing. "Does it smell like bananas in here to you?" he asked no one in particular. I glanced at Edith's purse, which I knew contained the culprit car freshener earrings.

All the way to the police station, Brian winced with pain as he tried unsuccessfully to peel the toupee off his head. When we arrived, various police officers stared at the toupee, then deliberately looked away. Brian fumed, humiliated.

"Actually, I had forgotten to prepare a talk," Nick quipped to the mission president. "This was all planned to get me out of speaking."

The mission president chuckled. "Nick, we've had some interesting times together, but this is the topper." Then he shared some stories about Nick's escapades at BYU, when the mission president was a professor there. Erica, Grayson, and Ryan stared at their uncle with even more admiration.

Then the police interviewed me and I explained how Kirk and Stony had originally tricked me and how they had learned of the fireside. "Believe me," I said, turning to my family, "if I'd had any idea who they really were, I would never have put the elders in danger."

"Or your family," Brian deadpanned.

I grinned. "Of course. And I just prayed that they wouldn't do anything in a crowd."

"That was good thinking," Nick said. "They probably were planning to follow me after the meeting and get me alone. Although, you can never predict what will happen when someone's carrying a gun." Nick explained that the agency had a file and pictures of these two, but Nick had never seen them in person. "I might not have recognized them without your note," he said.

"When I saw you coming up on the stand," the mission president admitted to me, "I wondered what on earth was going on. But something just told me to sit and wait."

Nick grinned. "Andy, why *did* you bring them up on the stand? I mean, that helped me immensely, but how did you think of that?"

I took a big breath. "I didn't." Then I smiled at the knowing faces of my family. "Someone else pulled me along and put the words in my mouth."

"That's how I ended up married to Andy," Brian said, as if he were still baffled by the entrapment. I elbowed him in the ribs.

"It was perfect," Nick went on. "The number two fear people have—after the fear of falling—is public speaking. By getting those guys to the mike, you shook their confidence and rattled their psyches."

"I did?" I thought for a minute, then smiled.

"And how'd you like their bow ties?" Edith blurted.

Everyone paused and smiled. "I knew you'd made them the minute I saw them," Nick said.

Edith beamed, then, almost shyly, bragged, "I gave 'em their haircuts, too."

Now everyone tried to smile and act impressed. "Well!" the mission president said. And then again, "Well, well!"

Brian whispered in my ear, "I guess the only thing worse than getting arrested, is getting arrested wearing a bow tie and a bad haircut."

"Shh!" I whispered back, "or having a red toupee glued to your head."

Next, the police talked at length with Edith, interrupted only once by Angel beeping like a microwave and shouting, "Pop Tart's ready!"

Soon we were climbing into Nick's limousine and heading to the hotel. I turned to Nick. "I'm sorry that I . . . I thought you were going to . . . kill the queen," I said to Nick.

We all fell silent, then everyone burst into laughter. "It does sound so ridiculous, now," I said. "But . . ."

Nick patted my knee. "Not when you consider the shady schemes you thought I was involved in all those years. Anyway, I forgive you. And the queen would probably be thrilled if she knew the danger you went through, trying to save her." He winked at Zan.

"Andy and Edith," Zan said, "I owe you one. You saved my husband and—" then she choked up. "No words can describe how grateful I am."

I gave Zan a hug, and Edith patted her knee. "You know what you need?" Edith said to Zan. "You need a good, crocheted handbag with your own initials on it. I'll make you one when we get home."

Zan froze on that thought, staring at Edith. I glanced down at Zan's Chanel handbag with two c's on it, then looked away, scrunching my lips to keep from grinning. Zan forced a smile, then cleared her throat. "How lovely," she said.

Brian was still tugging at the toupee. "I cannot sleep in this," he finally said. "Sister Horvitz, is there a solvent for this glue of yours?"

"I'm still working on one," Edith said.

"Great," Brian winced. "Nick, can we go to an emergency room or something?"

Nick smiled. "I don't know . . . I kind of like that look," he said.

Brian glared at him, and Nick knew it was getting too late to be yanking his brother-in-law's chain, so he directed his driver to find a hospital.

Zan frowned as she watched the driver turning down various streets. "I think we're going in circles," she finally announced.

"So. The male trait of refusing to ask for directions is an international thing," I said.

Brian goes berserk when I make this observation. "Hey," he said, his patience wearing as thin as his natural hair, "in the Council in Heaven, the men agreed to all be alike. When we came to the subject of what to do when we need directions, the unanimous vote was, 'Drive on.'"

"I remember that," Nick said. "The seminar was packed."

I nudged Brian. "And you were teaching it."

Finally, we pulled in to an "ambulance only" entrance and piled out. Zan and Edith volunteered to stay in the waiting room with Grayson and Ryan, who promptly dozed off on two sofas. Erica, Nick, and I went with

Brian into the examining room. Then two different doctors began prodding Brian's head, each marveling in
their British accents about what "jolly astonishing" stuff
they were observing. As one after another of their sol-
vents failed to dissolve it, one doctor said, "It's as if the
substance has a skinlike quality."

"Remarkable," the second one agreed.

"Come on!" Brian finally snapped, fed up with their
amazement. "Can you take it off or not?"

"Well," one smiled, "I've never scalped anyone before,
but if you're determined to remove this . . . this . . . "

"Toupee," Brian growled through his teeth.

"Yes. I suppose we can try to remove the epider-
mis . . . of course, we'll have to anesthetize it. And after,
you'll have to keep it properly dressed . . . "

Brian began sounding like Angel's impression of a
garbage disposal, a guttural roar simmering in his
throat. The doctors began scurrying, and after an hour
or so with razors and knives, they managed to scrape
the toupee away from Brian's head.

"There's only a little bleeding," a plump nurse said,
trying to comfort Brian.

"What bleeding?" he yelled. "I'm bleeding?"

"Please," a doctor said. "Try to remain calm. Bleeding is normal—"

"How do you know what's normal—you said you'd
never done this before!" Brian argued.

The doctors shook their heads and frowned at Brian's
un-British propriety. Then they gave him some antisep-
tic ointments, bandages, and a page of instructions to
follow.

"You're looking pale, dearie," the nurse said to me.
"Would you like to lie down?"

"And that's another thing," Brian interrupted, still
a good deal louder than necessary. "She's been fainting
and having hot flashes—"

"Brian!" I said. "That's private."

"Oh—and my skull is public domain?" Brian was
clearly losing his composure, yelling at anyone who

cared to join the conversation. His mother says he was the only kid in the world who had sibling rivalry without any siblings.

"Sir, please." The nurse nodded toward the rest of the clinic.

"Well, can you examine her?" Brian asked, as if I had no say in the matter.

"Excuse me," I said, rising from my chair. "But I believe that should be my decis—" and with that, I staggered, quickly putting my head between my knees until the dizziness subsided.

"She's also been throwing up," Erica said.

I sighed. Thank-you, Florence Nightingale. As if bringing one's husband in to be scalped is not enough embarrassment for one evening.

The nurse smiled and patted my hand. "A little blood test wouldn't be so bad, would it?"

I sighed, sat down, and rolled up my sleeve. "I hope you're happy," I said, speaking to Brian but refusing to look at him. "You just couldn't be the only one stuck with a needle, could you?"

"They're newlyweds," Nick said to the nurse with a wink. "Lovers' spats. You know." The nurse returned his wink, then headed down the hallway with my blood.

"If I'm fainting because I'm anemic," I said to Brian, "you have just made me worse." Then looking at him as he sat on the table with his head wrapped in white bandages, I couldn't help but smile. "You look so cute," I giggled.

Brian frowned. "I am wearing a hat for the rest of the trip."

"By the way, Brian, the doctors told me they got a peek inside your head," I grinned. "You're lucky. They didn't find anything in there."

Edith popped in just then. "How 'bout that glue?" she asked, the same way some people say, "How 'bout them Dodgers?"

"Pretty strong," Brian said, gathering all his strength to be polite.

Edith was all aglow. "Those doctors said they'd never seen anything like it."

"No doubt."

"They called it revolutionary."

Brian smiled. "Well, Edith, the Revolution means something different in England than it does in Ameri—"

"Brian," I interrupted, "I'm sure they meant it as a compliment." Edith smiled.

Just then the nurse returned and took me by the hand over to Brian's examining table. "Come, come, honeymooners," she beamed. I glanced at Nick, who grinned. Then she put an arm around each of us, and said, "Well, I think we can explain Mrs. Taylor's symptoms. You'll be happy to know that you're going to be parents! Isn't it wonderful? You're pregnant!"

18

MAKING HISTORY

Bands of amber sunlight sparkled in the prisms of the chandelier over our bed, then broke into rainbow flecks of color on the walls of our elegant hotel room. Nick had put us up at Claridge's, one of London's finest, old stately hotels. The kids were in an adjacent suite, and I rolled over to look at Brian.

Despite his skull cap, he looked gorgeous. "Just like a sleeping statue," I whispered, staring at my eternal companion as he slept in the early morning light.

Brian opened his eyes. "Andy..." he whispered and put an arm over my shoulders. "I had the weirdest dream. We were pregnant again."

I laughed. "I dreamed that, too. I even dreamed that you fainted, fell on the hospital floor, and had to be revived with smelling salts."

Brian remembered his scalping and gently touched his bandages. "How can this have happened?"

"Edith glued a toupee to your scal—"

"I don't mean *this*," he said, his irritation at Edith beginning all over again. "I mean the pregnancy." Brian was evidently still not over the shock of it. "How can we possibly be having a baby?"

"Well," I said, snuggling up against him, "first, I scooted really close like this—"

Brian just looked at me. "Aren't you too old or something?"

I sighed. It was one of those moments that require no response.

"I mean . . . one minute we think you're in menopause," Brian went on, "and the next minute you're becoming a mother again."

I smiled, thinking of the cuddly little pajamas, the lullabies, the tiny little diapers and socks.

"I guess this explains all your weird behavior," Brian said. "Well, not *all* your weird behavior." Then he glanced at me to see if I had registered enough annoyance. But I was still floating along in a dainty dream of pastel booties.

"Remember the look on the nurse's face when we woke up Grayson and Ryan and she heard them call you Mom?" Brian said. "She thought we had finally gotten married after having three kids!"

"A Kodak moment," I agreed. Then, thinking of the way the children had leaped with joy at the news, I said, "Oh, the kids are so excited."

Brian stroked my hair. "And how about you?"

"Oh, absolutely," I said. "I mean, I'm shocked. But . . . a baby, Brian!" Then I looked into his face. "How do you feel about it this morning?" Last night he had become virtually catatonic, the longest stretch of frozen panic anyone has ever seen.

Brian sighed. "Scared to death. I'm old, Andy."

I laughed. "You are not; lots of people our age are having children."

"They're having grandchildren," Brian corrected. "Just think how old I'll be when the baby graduates from college. Oh, man, college! How can we afford to send four kids to college?"

"They'll all be brilliant like their father, and get scholarships," I said, kissing him and pulling him close. "I'm so happy, honey."

"Four kids," Brian mumbled. "I just can't believe it . . . " Brian, an only child, thought we had a big family when Grayson was born.

"So you had no idea you were pregnant?" Brian asked, unaware that he had asked this same question eleven times the night before.

I smiled. "This time is completely different," I said. "I was sick night and day with the others. But this time it happens only sometimes. And I've never fainted before. I guess the symptoms change when you're—" I bit the bullet, "older."

Brian was drifting into a daze again. "Yeah," he mumbled. Then seeing that he had agreed with me at exactly the wrong moment, he blinked and shook his head. "Oh, honey, I didn't mean ... you know you're still my beautiful bride ... I ... " He sighed. "Can we start this morning over?"

I smiled. "Sure." Then I closed my eyes and pretended to be asleep again.

Brian kissed me on the cheek. "Good morning, my love. Are you feeling okay? How can I help you, darling?"

Well, I figured I'd better get it while I could, so I pretended to pout a little. "Hmm," I said.

Brian traced the curve of my cheek with his finger. "How can anyone so young-looking be the mother of four?"

I smiled. He was definitely on the right track.

"I'll bet all the little spirits up there are fighting over who gets to have such a gorgeous, wonderful mommy."

"Probably," I yawned.

"How about some room service for the new mommy-to-be?"

Brian pressed a button for the floor valet, who, like all the staff, wore tuxedo tails. Instantly, the valet knocked on our door. "Yes, Mr. Taylor, what can we do for you—some breakfast?"

Brian stammered. "Uh, yes. And a morning paper."

"Of course," the man said, as though our order had just made his day. "May we pick up any dry cleaning for you?"

Brian glanced back at me and grinned. "You like this hotel, don't you?"

"I got used to it after about two seconds," I said, leaning back on my pillow like Scarlett O'Hara, waiting to be pampered. Nick sure could pick 'em.

After he closed the door, Brian climbed up onto a table. "What are you doing?" I laughed.

"I would like to publicly apologize," he said.

"But there's no public."

Brian was not to be discouraged. "If there were a public, this is where I would stand and what I would say."

I grinned and sat up like a kid in pajamas enjoying permission to stay up late and watch television.

"I'd like to beg your forgiveness for being a poop about this new baby."

I laughed.

"My reaction must have disappointed you in the midst of your excitement over this fabulous news, and I apologize for being the family rain cloud," Brian said. "I hereby take back all my whining and self-pity. Will you forgive me?"

I laughed and clapped my hands. "Of course I will." As Brian climbed off the table, I said, "That was the best apology I've ever heard."

Brian gave me a tender kiss. "And the most deserved. Now. May I draw you a bath?"

After I had soaked in the extra-deep tub of bubbles and wrapped myself in a fluffy robe, room service arrived.

"Andy—look at this!" Brian shouted, holding up the morning paper. There, under the banner headline "MORMONS NAB TERRORISTS," was a huge photo of four English bobbies clutching Kirk and Stony by their arms, while Edith stood prominently in the foreground, aiming her glue bottle like a revolver. Left of Edith was Brian, a stunned expression on his face, a terrible toupee on his head, and a fainting wife in his arms. I looked drunk as a skunk. Nick and Zan were on the right, tastefully posed like some couple from the pages of *Town and Country* magazine.

"Look at my hair!" Brian shrieked.

"Look at your wife," I muttered. Then, trying not to bust up laughing, I said, "Now what thinking person wouldn't want to join the church and be like us?"

Brian was laughing so hard his eyes were watering. "This is the worst picture I've ever seen in my life!" He reached for the phone. "I've got to call the newspaper and see if they'll sell me the original. This is absolutely priceless."

"Oh no you don't," I said, pushing the receiver back down again. "You'll have this made into a poster and I'll never live it down."

"Poster, shmoster," Brian said. "This could be the photo on our Christmas cards! You can even see the kids faintly in the background."

"Forget it!" I shouted, holding the phone tightly in its cradle. Then it rang and both of us jumped.

It was Edith, calling—or I should say, shouting—from her room down the hall. "Hey, did ya see me in the paper?" Edith must have graduated from the mental hospital Summa Cum Loud. (Why use a phone at all? Why not just holler down the hallway?)

"Quite a photograph," I agreed.

"I think I just naturally attract media attention," Edith said. "I've always had a hunch that I'd be famous someday. Nick and Zan look nice, too." Then she paused. "But you folks look kinda truck-struck."

"Well, we've never been too photogenic," I said. Brian was sitting down to read the article, but looked up then and feigned astonishment.

"Call me when you hear from Nick about what we're doin' today," Edith said.

I promised, then dialed the kids and invited them to get dressed and come over to share our breakfast feast.

"Look at this," Brian laughed, almost choking on his orange juice as he read the details. "They couldn't make the kidnapping charge stick—at best it would be criminal fraud—I mean, nobody really forced you guys over here. And they had no proof that these guys were trying to kill Nick—the evidence in their car showed a link with Montoya, but there was no actual crime committed."

"What about carrying a concealed weapon?" I asked, wondering what was so funny, and worrying that Kirk and Stony would get free and come after Nick again. "You go to jail for that, right?"

"Right," Brian said, still laughing. "And most people get right out on bail."

I gasped.

"But guess why they denied bail in this case." Brian was laughing almost too hard to tell me, but finally said, "Macaws are covered under the Convention of International Trade of Endangered Species—it's a violation of British law to bring one in without documentation!" Brian was holding his sides, howling.

"What?" I shouted and scanned the article. Sure enough, Kirk and Stony were being held for investigation of smuggling in that crazy macaw. Angel turned out to be the hero of the day. The bird had been confiscated and was now in quarantine until its health could be checked. It turns out that members of the parrot family carry a poultry disease which England is not eager to see spread to all its chickens—Velogenic Discerotrophic Newcastle disease, of all things.

"Let Angel try to say that," I said.

"Wow," Brian mumbled, reading on about the disease. "Pretty grisly story about what happens when a chicken catches it . . . "

Ah. Another happy picture for Edith to describe while people are, say, eating.

"Look at this," I said, pointing to one paragraph. "Nick's the one who tipped them off about the poultry problem. That guy knows more about chickens than Colonel Sanders."

"Well, it worked," Brian said. "Not only will Kirk and Stony be slapped with a stiff fine, but together with the concealed weapon charge, it's giving the police enough time to gather additional charges of drug trafficking."

With Nick's help, officials felt sure they could put "two of society's biggest fugitives" away for a long time.

I grinned and read the rest of the article over Brian's shoulder. Edith was described as "an American inventor," the way you might label Thomas Edison, and her glue was described as "still holding as of three A.M." At this, Brian smirked and said, "See—now aren't you glad we went to the hospital?"

Nick, who dazzled the reporters from the minute they met him, was called a "first-class spy," and a sidebar story detailed his choice to retire and serve his church. A reporter even interviewed the mission president, who got in a few good words about our elders who leave schooling for two years to support themselves while serving the Lord.

"Finally," I said, "some good PR for the church in all this."

"Hey, read this part about when you discovered the evidence in Pennsylvania," Brian said. "They're saying it runs in your family to be a super sleuth." Paula and Natalie would just die.

"Check out these mug shots," I said, turning to the back page where the article continued. Edith's haircuts made the crooks look even scarier. It turned out their real names were Terrence Emery Kirkson and Ronald Galway Stone.

"Well, Terrence and Ronald, it's been great traveling with you," I said. "We hope you'll choose Montoya Airlines for all your business needs."

Brian laughed, then pointed to another article. "Look," he said, "the pilots' strike finally ended."

"Ah. Just in time."

Brian pulled me close, then suddenly looked into my eyes. "Hey—you don't suppose I hurt the baby when I tackled you in the garage that time, do you?"

I waved away his concern. "Are you kidding? Super sleuths like me . . . we live on the edge of danger."

Just then the kids came barreling into the room like starving Dobermans. Brian stared at the quickly disappearing breakfast. "I could have sworn there was a giant feast here a minute ago," he said. Then he whispered in my ear, "And you think we can feed another one?"

I laughed and demanded a good morning kiss from each of the kids, jelly-sticky mouths or not. Then Brian showed them the newspaper.

"Look at your hair!" Erica gasped.

Brian smirked. "Yes, but look at your mother."

"What is this—" I asked him—"Consolation in not looking the worst?"

Brian shrugged and smiled.

"Mom, you look dead," Ryan said.

"Please," I said, rolling my eyes. "Don't candy coat this, Ry. Just tell it how you see it."

"Okay," Ryan said, "you look worse than dead."

"Look at Sister Horvitz," Grayson said. "She'd make a good marshall." I could just picture Edith starring in the new TV western, "Nutsmoke."

"Just think," Erica said to Brian, "Before you were *teaching* history; now you're *making* history!"

Just then the phone rang again. It was Nick telling us to dress up in our very finest. "I have something special planned," he said, "and a driver will be there at ten o'clock to pick you up." I relayed the message to Edith, then stepped into the kids' suite to help them into their best clothes. When I came back into our room, Brian was just heading out. "I've got to buy a hat," he said.

"What for?" I asked innocently.

He smirked. "I'll be right back. Whatever this is, I refuse to go there looking like a giant Q-tip."

"Hey, I know," I said, "tie a red ribbon around your neck and you can go as a bowling pin!"

Brian scowled, then headed out.

Soon we were standing on the curb like a wedding party, awaiting our limousine. I had offered Edith a wool wrap I'd brought, since none of my clothes would fit her, but she had declined, preferring her "I Love New York" shirt, worn (of course) with the apple earrings and liberty crown.

"I hope it's a tour of London," Erica said as we drove along. "Uncle Nick said he'd show us all the sights."

"Look at all the pigeons," Grayson said, pointing out a flock of birds as they fluttered about a gleaming fountain.

Edith sniffled. "Makes me miss Angel," she said.

I squeezed her hand. "He'll be all right," I said. Then I thought, it's the people who have to hear him we should worry about.

Brian was snapping pictures of museums and monuments as we honked and bumped through London's busy streets. Erica, who had received a camera on her last birthday, was pressed up against another window, waiting for the perfect shot.

"Hyde Park," the driver announced, as we all threw ourselves to the other side of the car. It's a miracle it didn't tip over.

"Front gates of Buckingham Palace," the driver continued.

"Oh—Buckingham Palace," Erica said, rolling down her window and hanging out to get a better shot. "I was hoping we could see this!" She took a picture of the red-coated sentries standing guard.

Brian, too, was rolling down his window and snapping away. The driver turned the corner, then pulled up to a side gate. The guards looked in at us, smiled, and waved us through.

"Hey, isn't this something?" Brian said, turning excitedly back to me. "This guy drove right through the gate! Now we can really get some close shots!"

The boys and I grinned, thrilled to get such a close glimpse of this famous attraction. Eager not to miss this rare view, we were all hanging out the car windows,

Edith pointing to the upper windows of the palace and saying, "Betcha that's where the jewels are stashed."

Suddenly the driver stopped the car and got out.

"Oh, great," Brian said. "What a place to have car trouble."

But the next thing we knew, he was opening our doors and helping us out. "You're not leavin' us here, are you?" Edith said, squinting into the man's face. "Because I got high connections, and if you think you can just—"

"Edith," I said, pulling her gently away from the startled driver, "I think perhaps Nick has arranged a tour or something." Please do not glue this man's feet to the pavement, I thought.

"It's a photography stop," Brian explained to her.

"Oh." Edith reached back into the car for her purse and ever-present bag of glue bottles, while I shrugged my best silent apology to the driver. "I'd better take all this with me," Edith muttered. Then scoffing at the countless guards around the car, she said, "You never know how tight the security is at a tourist attraction like this."

"Good morning!" We all turned to see Nick and Zan coming toward us. Nick thanked the driver, then led us to the palace.

"Now for the surprise," Nick said. "Come with me."

"What?" Brian said. "But that's impossible. Only the Queen's Gallery is open to the public."

"Nick has special permission," Zan confided with pride. I put my arms around the kids as Nick led us through the majestic halls and beautiful furnishings of the monarch's residence. "Touch nothing," I hissed to the children. The queen was undoubtedly out of town, and this had to be Nick's last, grand finagle. A door closed behind us and I jumped, certain it was someone catching us on the premises, eager to throw us out.

"Are you sure we can be in here?" I whispered to Nick.

"Positive," he whispered back. "And you don't have to whisper."

"Cool," Grayson said, his voice echoing against the gleaming marble.

"Shh!" Then I turned to Nick. "I think we should get out of here," I whispered. "I'll bet they don't appreciate—"

Just then a tall man in formal attire appeared out of nowhere and introduced himself as an assistant of some kind. He then escorted us along, to what I was sure was a speedy exit. Well, at least he's being polite about it, I thought. That's more than I'd do if I caught a bunch of tourists prowling through my home.

Suddenly, the man pulled open two heavy doors, and there, with a small entourage, stood the queen of England herself!

"Great Scott!" Brian blurted. "I mean, Brit." Then he locked glances with me, his poor eyes filled with immense pain at the realization of what he'd just said. Immediately, he whipped his hat off his head and blushed crimson below his white bandage.

Graciously, the queen stood and smiled. "So this is Mr. Butler's family!"

19

MANOR MANNERS

The queen came right over to us, and shook our hands. "We are ever so grateful to your brother," she said to me.

I blabbered. "Oh, well, I, he, we, you, goodness, we're, heavens, just—thank-you." Then I returned Brian's glance of pain.

"It's great to meet you," Erica said, vigorously shaking the queen's hand. "These are my brothers, Grayson and Ryan." Brian and I stared. How did Erica get the corner on composure here?

Grayson and Ryan each shook her hand, and Grayson said, "You look just like the real queen."

She chuckled as Nick said, "Grayson, this *is* the real queen. You call her 'Your Majesty.'"

Grayson's eyes swelled round and he became, thankfully, speechless for the rest of the visit.

"We're so pleased you could be here for Mr. Butler's luncheon," a member of the court said.

"His what?" Edith bellowed, for once expressing the thought on all our stunned lips.

The escort led us to the dining table. "Please be seated."

"The queen is the friend of Nick's who we've been staying with," Zan confided as we settled into our chairs.

"You've been staying at Buckingham Palace?" Edith said, finally in a whisper. "And you put us up in that dump?"

Zan laughed, thinking Edith was joking. I glared daggers at Edith and motioned her to be quiet.

"Rarely does anyone stay at the Palace," an aide whispered to me. "But your brother saved Her Majesty's life a few years ago, and they've since corresponded and become extremely close friends."

I gulped, speechless.

The queen was saying something about "just an informal gathering." I stared at the gleaming table: gold-trimmed china, crisp white linen, sparkling crystal, and an ornate silver service. This is informal?

"I can't believe we were hanging out of the car taking pictures," Brian said, his face still red with embarrassment.

"I can," I said.

As lunch was served, the queen chatted and laughed with Nick; obviously the two of them clicked in one of those amazing relationships that no one in their right mind could ever have predicted.

I scarcely touched my salad or my roll because I was so intent on staring at my children and trying to communicate formal etiquette telepathically. Occasionally I would nod at a goblet, and one of them would place it in a less precarious position. If something broke, I knew I would die, and Edith would get to prove her point about the expense of shipping dead bodies from country to country.

"This is good!" Ryan blurted, taking a bite of halibut that he would normally whine about. Then he looked at me for approval. Obviously he'd been lying, but since it was for the sake of preserving his mother's life, I decided to let it go.

Various attendants and kitchen staff bustled about, taking care of our every need. As Nick and others spoke with the queen, I noticed many of them calling her "Mom." Evidently, Ryan had picked up on the same phenomenon, and finally asked, "How many kids does she *have*?" at which point everyone there burst into laughter.

Nick then explained that the first time you speak to the queen, you say "Your Majesty," and after that it's "Madam." In England, that shortens to a "Ma'am" that sounds like "Mom."

No one could have found the whole incident funnier than the queen herself.

We finished off our meal with berries and thick cream, and plates of shortbread cookies adorned with tiny violets.

After lunch, the queen stood and said, "We owe a large debt of gratitude to this man. He has served not only his country, but all countries of the world, with his fearless courage and determination to fight the war against drugs. We salute you, Nicholas Butler." She then presented Nick with a sterling silver platter, engraved: "To Nicholas Butler with great friendship and deep appreciation, Her Majesty the Queen of England, Elizabeth the Second, Head of the Commonwealth, Defender of the Faith."

I dabbed at the tears welling up in my eyes. What a wonderful tribute to my darling brother. So this was why he brought us to Europe—to share this great moment in his life. "Stop looking so shocked," I whispered, nudging our little group.

Next, the queen presented Zan with two gorgeous wool tartans as a wedding gift. Zan was as gracious and polished as a princess. Then, seeming to relish her role as gift giver, Her Majesty then asked Edith and me to come forward. "This is a small token of my gratitude for your work safeguarding England in last night's capture," she said, and handed us each a package containing exquisite English bone china. Mine was a stunning fluted bowl, and Edith's was a tea pot.

"Well, we're LDS," Edith began, heading straight into a discussion of why Mormons don't drink tea. To keep Edith from embarrassing the queen (and, okay, me and my family as well), I blurted, "so on behalf of our church, we'd just like to thank you for such a wonderful reception, and such exquisite gifts." Then I pulled Edith back to her chair in a fog of confusion.

"Some missionary you are!" Edith hissed to me. "You just blew the perfect chance to tell her about the World of Wisdom."

Edith is never at a loss for the wrong words.

As we all gathered around Nick to congratulate him and admire the platter, Ryan whispered—absolutely impressed—"This is like getting a medal from the fire department!"

I smiled.

Ryan tugged on my sleeve again. "But are we still Americans?"

I hugged him. "Of course, sweetheart."

"Whew!" Ryan said.

The queen overheard this interchange and chuckled again. "What a lovely family," she said.

"I'm just a friend," Edith piped up. "And an inventor."

"Yes," the queen said. "I read about your splendid invention just this morning."

Edith winked. "Well, today's your lucky day, Your Majesty. It just so happens, I brought a few bottles of it along with me! And I'll sell you one for ten bucks. Discounted, of course, you being royalty and all."

I sputtered, Brian stammered, Zan winced and Nick turned white as chalk. "Edith—" Nick said, stepping up into the bargaining arena. "I think Her Royal Majesty—"

"I'll take two," the queen interrupted. And before we knew it, Edith had sold the queen two of the green squirt bottles.

An aide counted the English pounds into Edith's palm. She stared at the unfamiliar money. "Hey, what kind of money is this?" she asked the aide. "You tryin' to pull a fast one?"

Brian, trying to quiet her, quickly whispered to Edith that he'd exchange the pounds for dollars as soon as we got back in the car. Edith made him promise, hold out his hands to make sure his fingers weren't crossed, then she stuffed the wads into her purse.

"Your Majesty," Nick said, trying to salvage the situation, "Please don't feel obligated to—"

"Nonsense," the queen smiled. "We ladies in crowns have to stick together." Then she chuckled at her own joke as Edith grinned and adjusted her own liberty crown.

"Now, you wanna watch out with that stuff," Edith said to her. "It's strong. Took this guy's scalp right off." She nodded towards Brian as if he'd simply been lugged along as a visual aid.

Brian's jaw was still hanging open, stunned at Edith's nerve, but he closed it as all eyes turned to him. "I . . . I have a hat," he mumbled.

As the queen bid us all good-bye, Erica said, "Boy, wait till my teacher reads what I did on my summer vacation!"

Edith wouldn't get back into the car until Brian made good his promise and exchanged her English currency for American. Brian then discovered that he only had a fifty dollar bill, which he snarlingly relinquished to the self-satisfied Edith. She then climbed into the car and patted her handbag. "Tidy little profit," she said.

I just stared. How on earth did she have the guts to bring glue to the queen of England? And *sell* it to her, yet!

Edith smiled at Nick. "Now where?"

Nick laughed as the car rolled out onto the streets of London. "How does France sound?" he asked. I gave Nick my best "Are-you-nuts?" glance, at which point he said, "After all, Sister Horvitz, you helped save my life."

I sighed. It was just like Nick to want to thank her by bringing her along for the rest of the trip.

"Nah, I'd better wait and see if Angel can get out of quarantine," Edith said. "Besides, I've got to go home and get ready for homemaking meeting. Maybe I'll go to France another time." (Like terrorists pop up all the time with similar offers of trips to Europe.)

"Now," Edith said, "I wonder if I can exchange this tea pot for something else." She glanced out the windows and looked around. "Where's a Wal-Mart?"

CHAPTER 20

THE HOME STRETCH

"You know," Nick said, as he arranged for Edith's trip home the next morning, "she's really a remarkable gal. And that glue is pretty phenomenal."

Brian declined to comment.

"She's certainly one of a kind," I agreed. I could only imagine what lay in store for the passenger who'd be sitting beside her on the return trip. She had changed out of her "I Love New York" gear and was now wearing enough souvenirs of London to open a gift shop.

As she headed down the ramp to the airplane, we overheard her bellowing to another passenger, "I met the queen of England yesterday—" as the passenger gave her a funny look and stepped quickly away.

"Poor Edith," Brian said. "No one will believe her."

"And she traded her only proof for an orange raincoat and a mood ring," Zan sighed, still amazed that Edith could part with a gift from the queen—tea pot or not.

Angel would have to wait and fly home—rather be *flown* home—in a few weeks after passing health exams and getting the import/export document mess straightened out. Authorities assured Edith that her bird would be well taken care of and treated like the hero he was.

The rest of the trip went without a hitch. Even the weather was postcard perfect. Ryan posed in front of Big

Ben with his arms matching the clock's face. Grayson was caught on film in Trafalgar Square, scattering a flock of pigeons. And Erica struck some dance poses beside a poster of the Royal Ballet.

Brian insisted on covering his bandaged head in hats from every region we visited. I came home with photos of him in England wearing a derby, in France wearing a beret, in Germany wearing a ski cap, and in Switzerland looking like Robin Hood, wearing a yodeler's cap with a sassy red feather tucked into the band.

"You look like you're trying to wear disguises," Erica commented.

"Unsuccessfully," Nick added.

At an outdoor café the day before we left, Ryan asked Erica to help him write postcards to his grandmothers. I was curious to see what highlights he would choose to mention—the drama of capturing Montoya's hit men, the news of another baby on the way, meeting the queen of England, the castles and museums, the scenery and cobblestones, perhaps. So I listened in.

"Dear Grandma," Ryan began, "Europe is old. It's at least seventy." I could just picture his nearing-seventy grandmothers reacting to this gem.

"Ummm," I interrupted, peering over Erica's shoulder and knowing "seventy" was already written, "Perhaps you should say 'seventy thousand.'"

"But it's not that old," Erica argued. She shook her head, stunned at her mother's ignorance. "And you're married to a history professor!"

With that, Brian entered the discussion. Smiling when he saw what Ryan had dictated so far, he suggested saying "hundred" instead of "thousand."

"But that doesn't make any sense," Grayson said, suddenly joining the Committee to Write Postcards. "You don't say 'seventy hundred.' You say 'seven thousand.'" Then he, too, shook his head in dismay at his numskull parents. "Sheesh!"

"How about seventy decades?" I suggested.

Erica squinted at me. "Nobody talks like that," she said. "Hi, I'm Erica Taylor and I'm one decade old."

I looked to Brian for help and sighed. "What do you think?"

He shrugged. "Send it. It's funny."

The kids stared at the postcard, then back at their dim-witted dad. "You think that's funny?!" Grayson asked. He exchanged stunned glances with his siblings before speaking for the group. "You guys have no sense of humor," he concluded.

"Let's hope our mothers do," Brian whispered to me.

"It's *my* postcard," Ryan said, finally reclaiming the object in question. "Cross out 'old' and write 'ancient.'"

"Oh, much better," I deadpanned, defeated by a five-year-old with an expanding vocabulary.

Speaking of expanding, I was quickly outgrowing my meager travel wardrobe. "I should have bought one of those New York muumuus with Edith," I said to Brian the next morning, as we dressed to catch our flight home. Luckily I'd packed some elastic waistbands, because buttons were out of the question, now.

"It's all the German pastries," Brian said. "I've got the same problem."

I just stared at him for a minute and waited for his memory to kick in. "Oh!" he said. "You mean because of the baby!" Then he blushed. "Yeah, that's how it is when I'm pregnant, too."

We hugged. "You feeling okay?" he asked.

"If I'm not, I won't admit it," I laughed. "One plane is enough to miss in my lifetime." We kissed, and I asked Brian if he had come to grips with having another baby yet.

He paused exactly one second too long. "Sure," he said.

"Brian..."

"Okay, I'm still scared to death," he admitted. "It's a big responsibility. I mean, I thought our family was just perfect with three kids, and I didn't even feel I was giving enough time to *them*. Then I think of how expensive it will be by the time this one is in college . . . "

"I understand," I said. And I meant it. For me, carrying a little being next to my heart started a loving relationship that overshadowed all Brian's practical concerns. I thought about the baby constantly because it was a physical part of me. But for Brian, who keeps a ledger of gas mileage in the glove compartment, this baby's bottom line was megabucks, whether it was velvety soft or not.

"You gave me a blessing," I said. "Maybe you should have one, too. I wish you could feel as thrilled as I do. I can't explain how, but I know we'll be able to do all we want for this child. We can give it a loving home and every opportunity, Brian."

He smiled. "You're exactly the kind of woman I always dreamed of marrying. Strong faith. Wonderful mother to our children. Great legs."

I laughed. "You nut."

All the way home on the airplane, Brian bounced between me and Nick. He was either trying to keep my stomach settled or thanking Nick (for the umpteenth time) for the vacation of a lifetime. Then Nick and Zan would get tired of him and send him back to me again. Why couldn't the seat belt light go on, I wondered.

"Would you just sit still?" I finally asked him. "You act like you've just eaten a pound of chocolate." I pulled my blanket over my shoulders and tried to go back to sleep.

"I can't," he said, his eyes watering and a huge grin on his face. "It just hit me."

"What just hit you?" I asked, my eyes half open in a groggy stupor.

"We're having a baby!" Brian shouted. "We're having a baby!"

My eyes zinged open as I realized he was shouting this to the entire cabin full of passengers. Several people began applauding and Brian wiped his eyes with someone's Kleenex.

"I cannot believe you are doing this," I whispered, sliding down farther into my seat.

"Congratulations," someone called out.

"Take a bow!" said someone else.

Brian was bouncing down the aisle now, shaking hands and being slapped on the back. "Stand up, Andy," he called.

I was ready to strangle him. Here I was, queasy from head to toe, feeling bloated and sleepy, my hair a mess, and Brian was telling me to stand up and take a bow in front of all these strangers.

"This is a fine time to finally get it," I snarled, as Brian pulled me unwillingly to my feet.

I waved weakly, looking alarmingly like my newspaper photograph. Brian was looking at me as if I were his brand new bride. He kissed me on the cheek, pulled away grinning, then kissed me again. Passengers clapped, as Brian said, "I'm so happy," his voice choked with emotion.

"You're so weird," I whispered and struggled to get back into my seat. "This has to be the most delayed reaction in history."

"Just think," Brian said, sitting beside me and leaning into my face. "We'll be a family of six!"

"You've been using your pocket calculator, I can tell."

"One more little munchkin to run up and throw her arms around me when I get home from work . . . " Brian was lost in a fantasy, now.

"You think it's a girl?" I mumbled, trying to scoot down under my blanket again.

"Did I say that?" Brian asked.

I sighed and closed my eyes. He didn't need me for this conversation. On and on he went, listing the joys of having another child. The trips to Disneyland, the trick-or-treating, the Primary sacrament programs, the Honor Roll, the camping trips (okay, some of these are exclusively *his* joys), the home run hits, the crooked, hand-made Valentines, the tiny little people in pajamas who climb into bed with you at four in the morning.

"And we can afford it," he said suddenly, as if arguing with an imaginary accountant standing in the aisle. He paused. "If this one is anything like the others . . ." (Yikes! I thought, we'll be in major trouble!) ". . . we'll be the luckiest family on earth," Brian said.

I sighed. I hoped he was finished.

"You still awake?" he asked.

"How could I possibly sleep?" I asked.

"Me neither," Brian said. "It's just too exciting."

"Yep," I said, and sighed again.

Brian patted my stomach. Then, after a moment, he whispered, "Am I a good father?"

I opened my eyes and smiled. "The best. If you don't believe me, ask the kids."

Now Brian was bouncing across the aisle and down a few rows to the children. Soon he came back beaming, tears streaming down his face.

"I take it they echoed my opinion," I said.

Brian nodded, unable to speak for a minute as he settled in and buckled his seat belt. Finally he wiped his eyes. "I always feel more emotional when we're pregnant," he said.

Thankfully, Brian's enthusiasm faded into calm contentment by the end of the trip. He even managed to doze off once or twice.

Nick's driver met us at the airport. As we neared our house, Brian and I both said, "Here we are—home!" to the kids.

"Jinx," Brian said to me.

I just stared at him. "You can't jinx me. I'm your wife!"

"Yes he can," Grayson piped up, as if holding the manual of childhood rules in his hands. "You can jinx anyone. And you don't get to talk, Mom, until Dad says your name and unjinxes you."

Brian just sat there, smugly enjoying such a concept.

"You can slug her," Grayson suggested to Brian, "because she talked."

"Grayson!" I said.

Brian laughed. "Andy," he said. "Now you're un-jinxed."

"There will be no more jinxing," I said. I glanced at Nick and Zan, whose unfazed reactions were in marked contrast to their responses three weeks ago. Obviously, a vacation with three active kids adjusts your perspectives.

There was no way to thank Nick and Zan enough for treating us to such an incredible vacation. We all kept hugging and kissing until I thought Ryan was going to die of Yuck Overload.

Then the kids discovered that no matter how exciting a vacation has been, it's always wonderful to come home to your old surroundings. They bounded up the stairs to their bedrooms as Brian collapsed in his favorite chair, and I went into the kitchen. Somehow it didn't feel cozy to me anymore. It felt like the scene of a crime—and it was. The chairs Kirk and Stony had sat in were still scooted away from the table, their fingerprints undoubtedly still on the chair backs. I shuddered and felt sick again.

"You okay?" Brian asked, suddenly behind me. "This is where they talked to you?"

I nodded.

Brian shook his head. "I can't believe they don't even scoot their chairs in when they get up from a table." Only Brian would make this observation. Or, possibly, Edith.

Brian saw that his joking wasn't helping me adjust to the odd feeling I had in this kitchen now. He glanced around, thinking. "You know," he said, "I think this kitchen could use a new coat of paint. And maybe those chairs you've had your eye on at the antique store would kind of dress up the place . . . "

Tears rolled from my eyes as I threw my arms around him.

"Mom," Erica said, dashing into the kitchen, I was just in the backyard and you should see what somebody did to the doggie door!"

Brian glanced over his shoulder at the tiny door that once held me snug as a mouse in a spring-loaded trap. "Oh, wow—" he said, crouching down at the door and running his fingers along the bent metal frame. "This looks like somebody broke in." Then he stood, assuming commander-in-chief posture, and said, "Okay, everyone. Check the house and see what's missing."

I swallowed. "Wait. Wait. Let's not panic, here."

"Mom," Erica said, infusing five or six syllables into my name, "we've been, like, robbed."

I took a deep breath and decided to confess. "It was me," I said. "I bent the doggie door." Oh, the pain of confession! I felt like Blimpie at a Weightwatcher's meeting, admitting that I had swallowed twenty-eight hamburgers in one sitting.

"You?" Brian asked. "But how?"

I then explained, amid theatrical squeals and giggles from Erica and cheek-chewing efforts not to laugh from Brian.

"Grayson! Ryan!" Erica shouted, "Come and hear this!"

I simmered, knowing I'd have to endure the telling of this tale yet again (and again and again, thanks to the indelible memories of my children).

"You lied to me!" Brian said, his eyes dancing with pleasure at the thought of catching me red-handed.

"I did not," I said. "I merely explained that the two men came over. I didn't say how they got in."

Brian grinned. "This is definitely going in my journal."

I smirked. "And if you go first, your journal is definitely going in the trash."

Brian smiled the same way he does when he plays chess. "I'll make copies and keep them in a vault." Next to that hideous newspaper clipping, no doubt.

Grayson and Ryan then entered the scene and heard Erica's hysterical telling of their mother getting caught in a doggie door. Worst of all, they didn't even question the possibility of such a ludicrous event.

We then picked up Gizmo from my mother. She had already read about the capture in the paper and had been telling all her friends about her heroic children. For months she hadn't believed that Nick had been a spy, but now that she read it in the paper, she was finally convinced.

As for Gizmo, he had only chewed up one pillow and a chair leg, a record low for him. Caruso the cat had thrown up only twice, Mom said, a score I had personally more than doubled.

Brian's mother called when we got back and wanted us both on the line to tell about the trip. "First of all," she said, "did you have a good time?"

Brian sighed. "Boy! Almost, Ma." He then told her about the terrorists, which she hadn't heard a word about.

"I miss all the action," she groused. "This retirement village is cramping my style."

Then Monica called to report that everything had actually gone smoothly while I was away. In fact, she hinted, things went even more smoothly than when I'm home. It is not a great comfort to discover that every leader's worst fear is true: You really are replaceable.

Then Lara called. Referring to her "Chicks at Church" fireside, she said, "I guess we aren't the only ones who have wild firesides!"

I laughed. "I guess not."

"Of course," she went on, "in both cases I notice Andy Taylor was involved." Both she and Monica were relieved that everyone was home safe and sound. Well, allegedly sound.

Next we heard from Claudia Lambert. She was in tears. Andy, I just can't do it," she sobbed.

"Claudia, what's the matter?" I said.

"I can't let you kill Curly."

If my phone lines were tapped, I was in major trouble.

"Who's Curly?" I asked. It sounded like a gangster from a James Cagney movie.

"Our pig," she said. "He's just the sweetest thing you could ever know. He's like a member of the family."

I covered the receiver and whispered to Brian, "She can't kill the luau pig because he's become a member of her family, now."

Brian smiled. "That's what happens when you let just anybody through your doggie door." Then he gestured as if I were a perfect example, myself.

I gritted my teeth at him, then went back to the phone. "Don't worry, Claudia," I said. "We'll find another pig."

"Well, that's what I was going to talk to you about," she said. "I just couldn't bear it if we served pig. It would remind me of Curly. Think how you'd feel if the ward cooked Gizmo."

I smiled. This was one solution to furniture destruction that I had never considered. "I understand," I said. "I wouldn't want anyone to cook Gizmo."

Erica, walking by just then, shrieked, "Who would cook a dog? That's sick! You're not letting someone cook Gizmo, are you?"

"Why does she think her mother is capable of such a bizarre act?" I whispered to Brian.

He shrugged sarcastically, an act only Brian is capable of, and grinned.

"Please," Claudia begged, still crying, "promise me you won't do it."

I sighed. Fine. We would have the first vegetarian luau in the history of ward dinners. "You have my word," I said.

And that's just what we did. One month later we had the best ward dinner I can remember. Tiki lamps and colorful streamers filled Monica's backyard, Hawaiian music filled the air, and delicious fruits and vegetables filled our stomachs. The Primary children sang Hawaiian songs and some of them even did the hula. Nobody said a word about Claudia's pig.

"I really miss Edith's tamales," Brian said as we climbed into bed that night. (She had offered to lend us the newly-returned Angel, to round out the tropical theme. But we convinced her that Angel needed a rest.) Despite the fact that this was the perfect occasion to wear her crocheted fruit hat, Edith herself was conspicuously absent. But she had an excellent reason.

Two weeks after we got home, Nick's pharmaceutical company bought Edith's glue formula for five million dollars, plus a percentage of the profits. Edith had become a tycoon overnight.

When they printed the label, it showed Kirk and Stony with their hands and legs stuck together, right under the bold lettering, "Stick 'Em Up Glue." On the back, it showed Edith selling her glue to the queen of England. Edith had left immediately on a world tour, promoting the product as their international spokeswoman. She's even writing a book called *Have Glue Gun, Will Travel*.

"They think she's a creative genius," Nick confided to me. "Everybody's citing examples of social misfits who gave us some of our best inventions."

I could only smile and marvel.

All her life, Edith had been careening toward fame like a meteor rocketing toward the earth. And now she had hit, leaving a gigantic hole behind. Naturally, she asked to be released from her calling to accommodate her new travel schedule. (No one has ever been as reluctant as she was to let go of a calling they love.) I finally understood the truth of the old adage, "Beware of what you want; you just may get it." I had thought I'd welcome the day Edith was released. Instead, I'd give anything to have her back.

"I miss her," I said to Brian. "She kept things so lively. Her ideas were so different . . . "

"I'd hate to try to fill her shoes," Brian agreed. "For one thing, they'd be socks."

We laughed because now that Edith's glue was a recognized invention, she was suddenly dragging all her other inventions out of a trunk and trying to market them. One was socks sprayed with a heavy coating of "liquid leather" that kept them from springing holes and that, Edith claimed, made socks so strong you could wear them alone and forget shoes altogether.

As for Kirk and Stony, they were convicted of so many international crimes it made you dizzy to read them all. Even Major O'Malley, the pilot, had come forward as a witness against them, to reduce his own sentence. Best of all, Colombia was only too eager to extradite Francisco Montoya, to face charges of bird smuggling and a host of other crimes. O'Malley had taped a phone call of Kirk's to Montoya while we were in Pennsylvania, in which Kirk mentioned the macaw. Montoya had approved of them taking Edith and the macaw into England, thus implicating Montoya for directing his employees to commit the bird smuggling crime while carrying out their work.

Edith and I received beautiful letters of thanks from the President. "Well, this is no tea pot," Edith had snapped. "For this I paid taxes?"

Then two months later, Brian and I went in for an ultrasound of the baby. We hadn't had one with the other kids, so we were terribly excited. Holding the video camera, Brian zoomed in on the blurs and bubbles wiggling on the TV screen. "Let's see . . . this looks like a . . ."

"A head?" I asked.

"Nope . . . it looks like a . . ."

"A foot?" I guessed again, completely unable to tell what the globby shapes indicated.

"No, I was going to say an alien of some kind," Brian said. The doctor, also staring at the screen, had as puzzled a look on his face as we had on ours. Then he smiled, leaned back in his chair and said, "Do you want to know what it is?"

Brian and I looked at each other with eager grins and nodded. "Can you tell?" I asked, excited.

"Oh, yes," the doctor said. Then he said the word that changed our lives forever: "Triplets."

THE END

The adventures of Andy, Brian, Edith, and the rest of the gang will continue in Joni Hilton's next novel, Scrambled Home Evenings.